Jack Frost, CEO

Juliet McKinley

Copyright

To my Mom, who is always my number one fan, and to my sister, who is sometimes a dumb goldfish but has great taste in sisters.
To my PA, Gwen- this book is ***literally,*** for you.

Prologue

Jack

"Foster."

"Jack! How are you, mate? Are you still mucking around in the States?" Gio's voice booms down the line, a stark change from his more subdued public persona.

I close my eyes, rubbing them with one hand. Gio Santoro, my old roommate from Oxford. I was in the business program, and Gio naturally gravitated toward music. An unlikely pairing. He took an overly serious, academic-obsessed student and dragged me into his world of music, light, and laughter—sometimes kicking and screaming.

"Gio! How are you?" I longingly glance at the quarterly report on my desk.

"I'm currently living and working in New York. Why do you ask?" Gio rambles on for a minute about the weather, how things have been going, and where his next tour will take him.

Making a snap decision, I close the report, since it appears Gio won't let me get off the phone anytime soon—not that anyone would ever accuse him of being quiet. Even in uni, he was always the life of the party, having never met a stranger. For someone like me, who had grown up an introverted only child of older parents, Gio's larger-than-life personality could be downright terrifying, even if it meant ensuring I socialized with other people at various get-togethers.

It takes a moment for me to realize Gio paused, and my gut tells me he's up to his old tricks. "Well, *amico di lunga data*. I need a favor."

Gio and his favors, albeit not frequently requested, always have a way of throwing my life for a loop. I can't afford to let Gio Santoro turn my world upside down again. The last time it happened was when I met Monica, and I most certainly do not need a trip down that particular memory lane.

"What kind of favor, Gio? I have to be honest. I'm swamped with work. My assistant went into early labor, which means early maternity leave. The agency hasn't sent a replacement, and I'm barely keeping my head above water here."

I spin around to look out across the New York skyline. I don't have time for this, but Gio never cares about time management. After Oxford, he went on to become a famous singer. Last I heard, he was in LA, dating the lead vocalist of a popular indie band from Texas that seems to be making waves on the music scene.

Daisy? Denise? Delilah. That's it. Delilah.

"Well, that's why I'm calling. Antony told me what was happening. It seems his daughter is in the States finishing her degree, but there's a hitch. She needs internship hours, but no company wants to accept her because she's due back in Australia by Christmas."

I grip my pen hard enough that the plastic protests. The third musketeer of our little group, Antony, was someone I considered a friend until I caught him one night with my fiancée, who promptly ditched me and married him.

"I didn't know he had a daughter." I pause and take a deep breath. "I didn't think Monica would let herself get pregnant. She never wanted kids with me."

"No. She's still as selfish as ever."

"What?" My head spins with the news.

"His daughter is twenty-four. Long story short, Antony got his high school sweetheart pregnant at sixteen, but he didn't know. Something about him transferring to a private school. She raised the girl on her own until she got into an accident and passed when the kid was only twelve. The grandmother was considered unfit due to her age and the fact she was living in a retirement community. Hence, the authorities contacted Antony, and he took custody."

I raise my eyebrows at this. I feel sorry for the girl. I can't imagine Antony as a doting father. It would force him to take time away from his favorite person: *himself.*

"Gio, I don't know..." The last thing I want is a family member of Antony's running around my business and reporting back to him, much less his daughter.

Antony and I haven't shared a conversation since the night I caught him with Monica a decade ago and I would much rather keep it that way. That doesn't mean I haven't kept tabs on him. A cynical part of me thinks this girl could be a spy sent to access my business. After all, rumor has it Antony had a bad year and lost several customers.

"Jack, the girl is desperate. She's at the top of her class and a hard worker. She needs a fair shake. In fact, she's in town interviewing at Goldberg's."

Sometimes I hate that I know him better than most. I can tell when he's putting on a public front. I can also tell when he's being sincere. And right now, Gio Santoro is as sincere as they come.

I grimace. Goldberg is a leech, and his last three assistants were paid off to prevent the sexual harassment claims from going to court. Despite my lack of regard for Antony, I would never willingly subject a female to Goldberg's advances.

"For fuck's sake. Don't let the girl go there. Tell her to come here. I'll interview her myself. I promise nothing, Gio." I keep my tone firm. "I'll interview her. If she is as competent as you say, she can be my new assistant until she returns home, and I'll sign off on her internship hours."

"Jack, you're the best! Thanks so much! You won't regret it!"

Famous last words. I'm sure I *will* regret this very much.

My leather chair creaks as I spin back around to my computer. "What's her name? So I can put her on the list at the reception." I open an email and wait.

"Maisie. Maisie Mitchell."

Chapter 1

Maisie

I stare up at the skyscraper blocking the afternoon sun. *How do they keep the windows so clean?* The entrance has one of those roundabout doors. I hate them almost as much as I hate the real things.

I'm still standing on the sidewalk, chewing on my bottom lip. I'm not feeling confident at all.

When Uncle Gio called, I couldn't believe it. I'd been turned down so many times, I'd just about given up hope. No one seems to think I can do the work before my visa expires. I can apply to extend it, but I have to return to Australia. I can't put it off any longer. I know it's my fault for leaving the hours to the last minute, but when you have to work two jobs just to keep the rent paid, food on the table, and classes covered, it doesn't leave much time for unpaid hours.

He was furious when he heard that Father wasn't paying for my schooling. I'm not fluent in Italian, but I could tell from his tone as well as the choice phrases he used that he wasn't being complimentary. Uncle Gio put money in my account immediately. Then he set about trying to help me find a place to get my internship hours so the last three years would be well-spent, seeing as I can't graduate without them.

So, now, here I am. Outside Foster Inc.

Uncle Gio said he went to school with the CEO, who's excited to interview me. I need a hundred and eighty internship hours on top of what I'm already working at my two current jobs. While the money Uncle Gio put into my account has helped, most of it went to paying off fees and costs for the end of my degree and some small loans I took out to pad myself between semesters.

I just need Jack to give me a chance. Uncle Gio says he will, but I can't be sure until it's offered to me.

Walking into the lobby, I gawk at the marble floors and silver ornate work. People in business attire scurry back and forth, files and papers in their hands. Uncle Gio mentioned that Mr. Foster has done well since leaving Oxford, but I didn't think he knew what that meant.

I approach the gleaming reception desk, tucking my hair nervously behind my ear. "G'day. I have a meeting with Mr. Foster?"

The clerk behind the desk looks at me, and I have to grimace. His gaze runs from the top of my blonde curls to the thrift-store flats I scored last week. "Name?"

"Maisie Mitchell? I was told to come right over."

The clerk taps on his keyboard without peering up again. I nibble on my lip. Maybe Mr. Frost is in a meeting, or perhaps he's changed his mind? Uncle Gio said Jack was a good man, but maybe he was wrong about him being able to help my situation.

The clerk slides a plastic visitor badge to me. "Here is your pass. You need to take the elevator to the twenty-third floor. Then go straight down the hall, fourth door on your left. Someone will meet you there."

"Thank you so much!" I grab the badge, head to the lift, and punch the button for the twenty-third floor.

I bounce on the balls of my feet. I'm more than a little nervous. Uncle Gio told me Jack and Father didn't get along but wouldn't explain why.

The lift doors open, and I'm greeted by a long hallway down the middle of what appears to be an extensive cubicle farm. I tug my hair nervously as all eyes land on me. Counting the doors to myself, I reach the fourth on my left and open it. Only to come face-to-face with the man himself.

Chapter 2

Jack

Where is this girl?

When the receptionist messaged that she was downstairs and on her way up, I expected her to be in my office momentarily. I glance at my watch and sigh. "Guess this isn't important to her."

I grab my coffee cup and stand from my chair to let my private secretary know I'm no longer willing to entertain this whole interview idea. I approach the door as the solid wood slams into my nose and coffee mug simultaneously, covering me in blood and leftover Americano. Cursing, I stalk back to my desk and drop my cup down, in an attempt to stem the blood flow from my nose.

"Miss Mitchell, I presume?" My tone is rough and curt, and I notice a slight flinch before she rushes up to me with wide eyes and a pale face.

"Crikey, I'm so sorry! Oh no, your suit! I knew I should have knocked—why am I always such a blundering idiot?"

By the time my eyes stop watering, and I can focus, all I can see is a wealth of blonde curls surrounding a face that lesser men would battle for. At knee-level in front of me while her hands desperately wipe at my suit with crumpled tissue and a—

"Is that a McDonald's napkin?" I ask as the girl shoves something in my hand.

"Sorry. Macca's was by the subway, and I stopped off this morning." Maisie gazes up at me. Her bottom lip catches beneath her front teeth as she swipes at my suit.

I clear my throat and step back, pulling a handkerchief from my pocket and pressing it against my nose. I walk behind my desk, needing the physical barrier between myself and this girl. I sit behind my computer and gesture to the chairs opposite me.

Maisie stands from the floor and perches on the edge of her seat. The vision of her on her knees, staring up at me, is stuck in my head. So I clear my throat again before I take her through the standard interview questions. Her tone is calm, relaxed, and collected. Her face a pleasant mask and her accent barely noticeable now. I find myself frowning. It bothers me that she's putting on a professional front.

I don't want to look at that too closely.

"So, Miss Mitchell. Gio tells me you are highly competent, a hard worker, and would be an asset to my company while you're still in the States. If all of this is true, then how, pray tell, have you not been able to complete the required a hundred and eighty internship hours in the nine months you were allotted? That is roughly five weeks' worth of work, eight on the outside." I take off my glasses, rest them on my desk, and steeple my fingers.

She ducks her head, and a cascade of blonde curls hides her face. She mumbles something, but I miss it.

"Miss Mitchell. I detest mumbling. Please give me the respect I'm due. Look at me and answer the question."

Her head snaps up, and red slashes across her cheeks. "I've been smashing out two jobs since I arrived. Between working to pay for rent, food, and classes, I didn't have the extra time. I would've finished earlier, but I need to sleep too." Her accent is thick, and the fire in her eyes threatens to consume me. I can tell she's annoyed. I fucking love it. Her blush deepens as she stares at her clenched fists. "I'm sorry. That was incredibly rude of me."

I wave a hand, dismissing her apology. I wanted an honest reaction, and I received one. "It was an entirely insensitive question on my part. Gio didn't mention that you've been working so much. So you still need to complete your requirements. Doesn't Antony—I mean, your father—send you money?"

She exhales and glances at the ceiling. Out of habit, I also glance up, even though I know there's nothing worth looking at.

"My mother died when I was twelve. The following year, he sent me to boarding school. I haven't seen him for more than a weekend at a time since then. Seems a daughter didn't fit into his lifestyle. One of the reasons I came to the States to go to uni was the distance. However, going against his wishes meant I was cut off. At the time, it seemed like a fair trade. Uncle Gio sent me some funds when he learned that Father wasn't helping to support me. However, I used most of it to pay off some loans." If possible, her cheeks turn an even brighter shade of scarlet, and she puts a hand up to each one, trying to hide them. "Why am I telling you this? I'm SO SORRY."

My eyebrows must be at my hairline when she finishes her story. I need to let Gio know about this. There is no way he knows the full extent of Antony's neglect. I bet Monica has something to do with it too, but I keep that thought to myself.

I take a minute to look at her again, not her honey-yellow hair or chocolate-brown eyes. I look deeper. Her skirt, while tidy, has been mended several times, and her white button-up is slightly baggy, as if she's recently lost weight. Her shoes on her primly crossed feet are scuffed, and I doubt it's because they're her favorite pair.

I rest my mouth against my interlocked fingers and study Maisie intently. She needs more help than she realizes, and while I could inform Gio and let him handle it, I've found that I want to be the one to care for her. This feeling is shocking, to put it mildly.

"Well, Miss Mitchell, if you were to come to work for me, you would have to give up your other employment. I need you to focus on your tasks and not worry about making it to another shift."

When she opens her mouth to protest, I hold up a finger to halt her.

"However, I do understand the cost of living. So, for half the day, you will be paid as my assistant at the going market rate for the position. You will log your internship hours for the other half of the day. If we have to do any traveling, I will count those as double hours, as there will be many situations that require my attention outside the office setting. Is this agreeable to you?"

Her eyes are as wide as saucers, and it appears all she can do is nod.

"Fantastic. Meet with Martha in Human Resources. She will provide all the information you need for your first day. Seeing as it's Friday, I will see you bright and early Monday morning. That will be all, Miss Mitchell." I gesture toward my door and turn back to my computer.

She stands from her chair, curtsies, and then walks out. I wait until the door closes behind her and laugh. I can't remember the last time I've laughed this hard. Shaking my head, I unlock my screen to email Martha.

Damn, if Gio doesn't have a lot to answer for.

After I hit send, my mind wanders back to Maisie—*Miss Mitchell*. She doesn't look like Antony. She must resemble her mother, and if that's the case, I can fully understand why my former friend was enamored with the woman in high school. I may hate Antony, but I refuse to let Maisie feel the effects of that hatred. It seems she's suffered enough in her life already.

Chapter 3

Maisie

I walk out of Jack's office in a daze. This was not how I expected the day to go when I woke up this morning. Back at the lift bank, I realize I don't know where I'm supposed to go, and I don't want to go back and bother Jack—I mean, *Mr. Foster.*

I groan inwardly. *Did I really curtsy?*

I look around and see a girl sitting at a desk. "Excuse me? G'day. I was wondering if you could tell me where to find Martha? I was told to go talk to her."

The girl looks up at me and grins. "Welcome! Are you a new hire?"

I nod my head, and she claps.

"Fantastic! We need more women around here. It's a bit of a sausage fest, if you know what I mean."

The man in the cubicle next to her leans back. "You know, Stella, if you're looking for some sausage..." He wiggles his eyebrows suggestively, and the girl I now know as Stella lobs a rubber band at him.

"Ignore Jeremy. He's a moron. His mother dropped him on his head as a baby. It's the only thing that explains why his head is so big, but he's dumb as rocks."

"Hey!" Jeremy protests before sticking his tongue out and returning to his work.

Stella refocuses on me with a smile. "So. You need Martha. She's on the fifteenth floor. Why don't I just show you? I have a break coming up anyway. Hey, Jer? I'm going to take my friend here down to see Martha. If you see Mac, let him know, okay?"

Jeremy waves a hand to us, and Stella gets up and leads me back over to the lifts, pushing the correct button before we step inside.

"So. What do you do? Analyst? Accounting? Runner?" Stella pops her gum as the car descends.

"Um, I'm going to be Jac—Mr. Foster's assistant. Apparently, the last one went into labor early, and he's been unable to find a replacement." I tug on my curls, unsure if what I shared was privileged information.

"Oh, lucky! Mr. Foster is considered the most eligible bachelor in town, and you get to work with him daily!"

The lift opens onto the fifteenth floor, and I follow Stella into an office with a line of doors.

"That accent is different. Where are you from?"

"Oh, I'm from Australia. I'm here temporarily. I'll return home at Christmas, but this gives Mr. Foster time to find a suitable replacement. Apparently, he's been in the weeds." I pull my bag closer to my side, trying to pay attention to the turns we're making.

"You're going to have every guy in a five-mile radius chasing you with that accent. It doesn't hurt that you look like a Disney Princess either." Stella twists a lock of hair around her finger, almost like she's up to something, but then she twines her arms through mine. "I've decided to be your unofficial welcoming committee. Anything you need, let me know. This is Martha's office. See you Monday!"

I watch Stella walk away for a few minutes. She pauses, turns back, and waves before I can't see her anymore. Swallowing, I pivot on my heel and knock on the door in front of me. I've learned my lesson: *Always knock.*

"Come in."

I open the door to a tastefully decorated office. Martha, the lady behind the desk, is older with laugh lines gracing her face and a friendly smile. I instantly like her.

"Well, hello! Mr. Foster told me to expect you. Did you get lost?" She pushes up from her chair and comes around the desk, ushering me into her office and over to a seat.

"Oh, well. Mr. Foster didn't tell me where to find you, so I had to ask for help. Stella brought me down here." I gesture behind me as if the girl's still standing there instead of several floors down by now.

Martha chuckles. "That imp. She's a handful—that's for sure. She runs rings around all the other analysts. You could do worse for a friend. Now. Let's get you situated. Mr. Foster said you were here on a work visa? I assume you have all of that with you?"

I nod, gesturing to my bag, and the woman beams.

"Fantastic!" She takes my employment packet from me and starts copying the documents. "Fill this out, dear, and we will set you up with a badge. Do you have a car?"

My eyes widen. *Am I meant to have a car?*

But Martha just continues to smile. "No? Then we will get you a pass for the subway. It's company-provided, so no worries. I'll show you the canteen, which is accessible to employees 24/7 so help yourself. If you take the last of something, please do not leave the empty container. That is just good manners, my dear."

My head is spinning as Martha prattles on about the amenities. I don't plan on needing any of them, so I'm not too worried about absorbing the information right now. I could also always ask Stella when the time comes.

"Here is your compensation contract. Please read over this carefully, and if everything is as you discussed with Mr. Foster, please sign." She hands me a clipboard, and I nearly swallow my tongue.

This number cannot be correct.

"Excuse me, I think there's a mistake." I show Martha the clipboard, pointing to the section where my monthly income is listed.

She picks up a pair of spectacles and perches them on the end of her nose. "No. That's correct. That's the going market rate for this position. Is it not enough? Did you discuss a different compensation target?"

"No. Mr. Foster said it would be the market rate for the position. I just wasn't expecting the number to be that high."

"Ah, well. Mr. Foster is very demanding and pays top dollar for talent. Don't get me wrong—you will earn every penny—but he is also very understanding."

I sign and pass over the compensation contract and receive my badge and a packet of paperwork in return.

"Now, everything we went over is in that packet and you already have your badge. As Mr. Foster's personal assistant, your start time will be seven sharp. He's usually here around six. When you arrive, you should immediately print his daily schedule. Go over it with him and then make any adjustments he requires. Throughout the day, there will be last-minute accommodations, which means you will need to change the schedule accordingly. However, this initial meeting first thing in the morning is the most important and will set the tone for the rest of your day."

I stare at her like a deer in headlights.

She pats my hand comfortingly. "You'll get it quick, dear. Promise. Now, you're done with me, but if you have any questions, please do not hesitate to reach out. My email and extension are in your packet as well. Enjoy your weekend!"

I gather my paperwork, shake Martha's hand, and walk out the door.

What just happened?

I clutch my papers tighter to my chest. I got the job and will still get paid—more than I've ever been paid in the States. When I reach the sidewalk, I look around.

Maybe this is finally working...

Chapter 4

Jack

“This isn’t working.”

I look up from my Americano to see my new assistant standing in my doorway. Her long blonde hair is in a tight bun, her glasses perched on her pert nose. Her skirt is long enough to be proper but tight enough to show that she either wears thongs or nothing at all to work. I clear my throat as my mind wanders to what she may or may not be wearing under that skirt.

“What is not working, exactly, Miss Mitchell?” I glance at my computer screen and notice it’s only 6:15 in the morning. “You’re not scheduled to clock in for another forty-five minutes.”

She waves a dismissive hand and walks toward me with a clipboard. “Yes, but Martha said I could come in early. Now, what isn’t working is your schedule. You’re double-booked half the day and have meetings with clients that should be delegated to other departments. I’ll have to completely redo your entire calendar, and I want to know which appointments are a must-have for today.” She extends the clipboard to me.

I glance down at the piece of paper and realize she’s correct. I have double-booked and agreed to meetings where my attendance shouldn’t be mandatory. Sighing, I rub my face before ticking off six appointments I know I can’t possibly push. Then I hand the clipboard back, and Maisie glances over the pages.

"Okay, I can work with this. You have a dinner reservation with Amberly at La Bella Vita tonight." She lifts the top sheet. "Do you want to keep this or move it?" Maisie clutches the clipboard to her chest and stands there attentively.

"Tell Amberly I will meet her, but I won't be able to stay for dessert. She is more than welcome to order and put it on my tab—she's going to anyway. Also, my mother's birthday is this week, so if you could arrange for a bouquet of white roses with lilies to be delivered. The address should be in the system and block out next Saturday afternoon. I won't be available for work. I'm going to spend my mother's birthday with her. That will be all, Miss Mitchell."

She turns and walks away, and when I catch myself staring at her ass, I force myself to go back to my emails.

I'm forty-five pages into the quarterly projections report when my doors open again. I look up and realize I've been working—uninterrupted—for hours. Shaking out the knots across the top of my back and shoulders, I jolt as a tray containing a club sandwich, a side salad, and a fresh Americano is placed on my desk. More specifically, on top of my report.

"You know, I never understood Yanks and their Americanos. You're ruining good espresso."

I peer up, meet my new assistant's twinkling eyes, and swallow roughly. "Miss Mitchell, there is nothing wrong with an Americano. What happened to my schedule? I thought I had several meetings before lunch." I pull my report from beneath the tray and set it aside.

"You marked that you wanted to keep meetings with Hastings, Fellows, three board members, and the leads for four projects. Hastings is sick. He canceled. The meeting with Fellows is scheduled for one—so you need to eat that sandwich now—and the board members had questions about dividends. I asked if I could resend the reports they'd already received, according to previous calendars, and that took care of that. Your meeting with the team leads is now a joint meeting, as they are all having issues behaving like adults. And thus, they will not be treated as such. I will be in this meeting to take notes and ensure the projects are on track."

She delivers that last line while I'm midbite, and I immediately start coughing as the sandwich goes the wrong way. Maisie rushes behind my desk and pounds me on the back with way more force than I anticipate.

I wave her away and sip my coffee before reaching for my napkin. "What do you mean *not behaving like adults*?"

"Well, each of their projects hinges on the part of the other, and no one wants to take responsibility for why they are six weeks behind without notes or justifications for the bottleneck. So, since no one is keeping up with the required documentation and no department wants to accept responsibility *or* offer a solution to get back on track, they can discuss it with you as a team. I see no reason for them to flood your calendar with multiple meetings that will essentially all be the same, but with different teams throwing each other under the bus."

She gestures for me to eat while I'm trying to pick my jaw off the floor. "What did you say your degree was in again, Miss Mitchell?"

"I didn't, but it's in business administration." She turns and walks out the door, and I'm stuck staring after her, wondering what the hell just happened. In less than twenty-four hours, this girl has completely turned my company on its head. And I couldn't be happier.

Chapter 5

Maisie

The phone on my desk rings the second I sit back down after taking Jack his lunch. "Foster Inc., this is Maisie."

"I need to speak to Jack." The feminine voice on the other end of the line is brusque and borders on rudeness.

I wrinkle my nose. I have a few pet peeves, but being rude is at the top. "I'm having a wonderful day. Thank you for asking. However, Mr. Foster is not available. He is in a lunch meeting. Can I take a message?" I keep my tone polite despite sticking my tongue out.

"Listen, you put him on this phone right now and tell him I will not be ignored like this! How dare he think he—"

That's all I hear as I set the receiver on the desk and pick up my sandwich. Peanut butter and jelly. My go-to, cheap and filling lunch for the last several weeks. I take a bite and chew while the shrew on the other end of the line continues to rant and rave. Stella walks up to my desk as the lady on the phone goes silent. I pick up the receiver and hold up a finger.

"Ma'am. As I previously stated, he is in a lunch meeting and unavailable. I will tell him you called." I hang up and go back to eating my sandwich.

"You didn't take her information," Stella points out.

"I did not." I finish up my little sandwich before sweeping the crumbs into the trash.

"How will you let Mr. Foster know she called if you didn't get her information?"

"Oh, I have a feeling I don't need it."

Jack's door opens to prove my point, and the man in question walks out. He pulls up short when he spots Stella standing by my desk.

"Mr. Foster, a woman called—quite irate—and stated she will not be ignored. Unfortunately, that was all I could get out of the five-minute rant she left for you."

Jack grimaces. "That's Regina. Next time, hang up on her. I thought she would have given up by now. I broke things off with her months ago. She needs to get over it. It was just a few dates. I'm heading to my meeting if you want to take lunch before the team leads show up for their scolding." His lips quirk, and I smile back.

"I'll be there, sir." I stand as Jack walks past while nodding his greeting to Stella.

I smirk. "Told you. Now. What can I do for you, ma'am?"

"I came to steal you for lunch. And judging by that sandwich you just finished, it's a good thing I did. C'mon. Press *forward* on the phones and let's go to the canteen. I'll give you a mini tour while we're at it."

"Oh, but I—" I start to say, but Stella cuts me off.

"Nope. You heard the boss man. Go to lunch, and not that sad sack lunch you just choked down. Let's go. Grab your purse." She hooks her arm through mine and drags me to the lifts to the second floor. The doors open to a cafeteria-like setting with heaps of popular food options.

"Okay, each station has several items in your compensation package—it varies. They also have upgrade options that you can purchase using your badge, and the cost will be deducted from your next check. What tickles your fancy?"

I glance around the canteen, spotting Dasi Sushi. Never one to pass up a good California roll, I point, and Stella follows me. I grab a Cali roll and a Maki roll, and we sit at one of the many open tables.

Maybe I should go back and read the packet Martha gave me after all.

"So, it's your first day. Are you doing okay up there on your own?" Stella pops a piece of sushi into her mouth and chews, her head bouncing back and forth while her ponytail swishes from side to side.

"Yeah, it's a bit of a mess, which is to be expected."

Stella bobs her head in agreement.

I grab my own piece of sushi and dab it in soy sauce. "I know I have a lot to learn, and tons of stuff to sort. I have a feeling I'll be swamped for several weeks." I jump as a tray slams down next to us, and Jeremy plops into a chair by Stella.

"Yo, ladies. What does it do?"

Stella rolls her eyes and grabs another piece of sushi. "Jeremy, I don't remember inviting you."

"Jer Bear needs no invitation when he sees a pair of fine fillies such as yourselves sitting alone." He grabs a fry off his tray while wiggling his eyebrows suggestively.

"The fact that we are sitting together negates your logic that we're sitting alone, you goober." She steals a fry off his tray.

Jeremy just shrugs while grinning from ear to ear. "So, Maisie, it's your first day. How are you finding things at Foster Inc.?" He takes a massive bite of his burger, bulging his cheeks.

"You're too late. She's already answered that question. Has Mr. Foster said anything about assigning more project leads? We lost three to competitors, and they haven't been replaced." Stella sips her iced coffee and looks at me expectantly.

Shrugging, I take a sip from my bottle of water. "Nothing's been said about assigning or replacing new project leads from outside sources. The meeting today is with *current* project leads. However, I still have a lot of documentation to review and straighten out, so I should get back to my desk." I pick up my tray when Jeremy stops me.

"I'll bus that for you, Maisie."

Stella mimics him, but I smile, thank Jeremy, and return to the lifts. My finger hovers over the button when I hear a voice behind me.

"So, you're the one who stole my job."

I turn around and am greeted by a tall, slender redhead dressed from head to toe in designer labels with a pair of red-bottom shoes. I'm instantly pissed. I know a queen bee when I see one, and this particular one is a capital B.

"Oi, sorry, mate. I don't know what you're talking about." I try to play up the clueless foreigner act. Which typically defuses most tense situations.

"Oh, fuck off, Lucy. The job was never yours, and you know it. Don't try to pin the fact you didn't get a job you thought you deserved on Maisie. No one ever said it was yours." Stella comes up behind the girl and knocks on her shoulder.

"Watch it, Stella. That job was mine. I deserved it!"

I'm surprised Lucy doesn't stamp her foot to accompany her tantrum.

"Puh-lease, Lucy. You are barely qualified for the job you have. Besides, we know the only position you want is on your knees in front of Mr. Foster."

Lucy screeches, and the chatter in the canteen lowers drastically as she lunges at Stella. I step forward with my arm raised to shove her off when a booming voice rings out.

"That. Is. ENOUGH!" Jack bellows, and the resulting silence is deafening.

Chapter 6

Jack

The elevator doors open enough for me to see a skinny redhead let out a god-awful screech. And lunge. Toward Maisie.

Not on my fucking watch.

I'm livid as I step off the elevator, moving between the three women. Stella, the raven-haired girl with a wicked sense of humor, stands next to Maisie, while the screeching redhead stands across from them looking like she's sucked a lemon.

"What is the meaning of this?" When no one moves to speak, I turn to Maisie. "Miss Mitchell?"

"Well, sir, it would seem that Lucy has taken offense to my position as your assistant. She was under the impression that she deserved the job." Maisie refuses to look at me, and I dislike that.

"Is that so?" I murmur, glancing at the woman in question. I don't remember seeing her CV, and I would have, as we always try to promote from inside first. "Let's all go talk to Martha then, shall we?"

Lucy pales, and I smirk while gesturing a hand toward the elevator doors. All three women silently follow me inside. Maisie's finger hesitates over the buttons. Stella steps in and handles the situation. Truth is, I couldn't care less who gets us there as long as Maisie's safe. We arrive at Martha's office, where we find her texting furiously on her phone.

She glances up, her irritation evident by the way her mouth draws down. "Ah, there you are. My office, ladies. Now."

All three women follow behind her like meek schoolgirls while I pull up the rear. I've known Martha most of my life, and I can't say I've ever seen her overtly upset by an employee's actions. I know I'm sheltered from most aspects of human resources, but Martha keeps me in the loop when necessary.

"Now. Speak." Martha sets her phone down on her desk, piercing each girl with a pointed glare.

All three girls start talking at once, and I whistle loudly. "Maisie. You first." My voice is quiet in the resulting silence.

"I just finished lunch with Stella and was returning to your office to prepare for the two o'clock meeting," Maisie explains.

"Which we are now late for," I interject.

Maisie nods in acknowledgment before she continues. "I pressed the button for the lift when this woman..." She points at the redhead. "...came up behind me and accused me of taking her job. Stella rushed over to see what was going on. Words were exchanged and Lucy tried to strike Stella in retaliation. Then Mr. Foster showed up and, well, here we are." She shrugs and falls silent again.

"Is that true, Miss Masterson?" Martha taps her pen on the desk, where she is taking notes, as her glare lands on Lucy.

"That position was supposed to be mine!"

I wince at the shrillness of her voice.

"Miss Masterson, as you were previously informed when you applied for the assistant position, you lacked several major requirements for the job posting. You were made aware of these deficiencies and removed from the candidate pool. The position was never yours. Therefore, no job has been stolen from you, and if you truly believed that was the case, you should have come to me. We do not confront our coworkers in the canteen, and we simply do not attempt to assault them!"

Martha is standing at this point, her jaw set hard while the rest of her appears to vibrate with her anger. Then she smooths imaginary wrinkles from her skirt as she tugs the hem down.

"Miss Mitchell, Miss Jarvis, you may return to your stations. Have a seat, Miss Masterson." The Martha in front of me is one I haven't seen very often. And, frankly, she's terrifying.

I grab Maisie by the elbow and escort her out of the office. "Miss Mitchell, I need you to bump our project lead meeting at least an hour. Then I want you to pull any information from the system about whatever Miss Masterson was working on. I believe you have access to those files."

"I'm a part of that team, sir. I know the status of all the projects," Stella interjects while raising her hand.

"Very well, Miss Jarvis. I want you to gather all the documentation and then meet with Miss Mitchell to see what permissions you need to take over those tasks. That is all." I dismiss the girls and return to Martha's office.

I can hear Lucy even with the door closed. Sometimes being the CEO really, really fucking sucks.

Chapter 7

Maisie

Stella grabs my arm and drags me back to our stations. Once we're safely behind the closed doors of the lift, she starts to freak out. "Oh my God. Oh my God. Oh my GOD! DO YOU KNOW WHAT JUST HAPPENED?"

My head snaps back and forth with the force of Stella shaking me. "Yeah, mate, I know what just happened. You gave me a concussion!" I pry her fingers off me and step to the side. "If you're referring to what happened with the redhead—who was being a bitch—then no, I do not know. She's obviously gotten herself into a bit of a spot. That was totally not cool of her. She was going to attack you!" I straighten my sweater and skirt.

"I forget you're new. That's Lucy. She came here a year ago and has already been made senior analyst. That's unheard of. And it's only because she had half of the management bamboozled. She claims other people's work as her own while fucking the other half so they don't care. To make matters worse, she's had her sights set on Mr. Foster since the assistant position opened. She bragged that she would be the new assistant when you showed up. I don't know why she thought she was going to get it."

Stella huffs and I continue to listen to her rant.

"I mean, you heard Martha. She isn't even remotely qualified. Besides, she only wants the position because she's been trying to get Mr. Foster to notice her for the past year." Stella pulls me closer and whispers, "They call him Jack Frost, 'cause he's cold as ice in business. You haven't had a chance to see it yet. But the man can be RUTHLESS. Also, for some reason, Mr. Foster hates Christmas. Oh, he does the usual holiday stuff for the staff, but he never attends, never decorates, and never-EVER-EVER," she stresses, "wish him merry Christmas. We had an intern mess up one year, and he made her cry. She asked to be transferred to a different floor and everything. It was a mess."

"Okay, so I get that business part. Mr. Foster is pretty intense, but how can someone hate Christmas? The sand, the beaches... it's twenty-five degrees and hardly ever rains! We spend all day playing beach cricket and surfing, and—" My words die off when I notice Stella staring at me. "What?"

"How are you playing on a beach in twenty-five degree weather! Isn't it freezing?"

"Oh, no. Twenty-five Celsius. For you Yanks, that's like—" I do quick math in my head. "Seventy-seven. It's really quite warm over Christmas at home. It's one of the reasons I want to be back by the holidays. I do not handle the cold well. I miss my warm and sunny beaches."

"You haven't returned home since you moved here for school?" It was an innocent question, but it still landed like a kick in the guts.

Stella didn't know and I would never tell her that I didn't have the money to return home, even if I had been invited. Busy traveling the world with my stepmother, Father couldn't bother to send me money to live on, much less to travel back to Sydney for the holidays. The only person who would have wanted to see me would have been Nan, but she isn't doing well at all, which is why I have to be back this Christmas. No matter what. She needs me. Father dropped her in that care home and forgot about her.

"Well, there wasn't much point in going home. Besides, international travel around the holiday is notorious for issues, and I couldn't risk missing classes. I don't see how you Yanks can stand living here. Snow is a NO for me. If I never see snow again, I'll be happy."

Stella laughs, like I was hoping she would, as the doors open on our floor. "Let's talk to your manager about what Mr. Foster wants you to gather. I'll be at my station when you're ready."

Once I return to my desk, I update the project managers about the meeting being moved. I push Mr. Foster's remaining calls for the rest of the afternoon and then collect all the project files I can find in the system with Lucy's name on them. There are quite a few, and each project is managed by the same man, Kevin Smith. I make note of this before leaving the files on Mr. Foster's desk.

Stella shows up with her own notes, and I set about typing them out and arranging them in order. I'm not sure what Jack plans to do with all these projects, but I do hope that he gives a few of them to Stella. She seems to know her stuff, even though she's one of the junior analysts, along with Jeremy, Martin, and Paul.

I pop into Jack's office once everything is neat, ready, and annotated. He still has not made it back from HR—which is worrisome in of itself. When he returns, I want him to have everything he requested.

I notice the clock and nip over to the machine on the sideboard. Based on what I've read, Jack usually has an Americano about now. I've never made one. But it can't be that difficult, can it?

The machine gleams in the sunlight, and I swear it's as tall as I am with all these different buttons and levers. I swallow roughly.

I can do this. I can make a stupid coffee. How hard can it be?

Chapter 8

Jack

I roll my neck, trying to remove the kinks, and finally return to my office. Lucy had quite a bit to say about my hiring and, consequently, my firing decisions. Unfortunately for her, I don't give a fuck. The girl was delusional if she thought she'd ever be my assistant, especially after Martha had already told her she was not qualified.

Besides, I have Maisie, and she's turning out to be a fantastic assistant. Gio was right when he said she was a hard worker. She may have only started today, but she already made a difference in the way my office is run—for the better.

I'm mentally reviewing my calendar, so I don't notice that Maisie isn't at her desk. Until I open my office door and find her in what appears to be a life-or-death match with my espresso machine. Coffee beans litter the ground while bits and bobs of metal and plastic are strewn across the countertop.

Maisie glares and points at the machine, her glorious curls sticking out at various angles. "You think it's funny, don't you?" Her Australian accent is thick. The machine is quite understandably silent, which only seems to frustrate her more. "Listen, mate, if you don't start cooperating, I will give you a good kick."

I clear my throat, trying not to laugh as I interrupt my assistant's tirade. Her back goes ramrod straight, and as she slowly turns to face me, I erupt into full belly laughs. Maisie has wet splotches on her shirt, coffee grounds in her hair, smears on her cheeks, and the portafilter in her hand.

I stride up, taking the portafilter away, and she blushes a pretty pink. Without thinking, my hand reaches up and gently swipes the coffee from her cheek. Her skin is warm under my touch, and I find myself cupping her face for longer than is work-place appropriate.

Her wide brown eyes stare up into mine, her pupils blown wide as her breath quickens and her pink lips part. I slide my hand into her hair, my fingers tangling in the silken strands before tugging slightly. I catch her gasp with my mouth above hers. I'm staring into her eyes as I brush against her lips.

My cell phone rings, breaking the moment, and Maisie jumps back while pressing a shaky hand over her lips. She turns and dashes from my office. I curse under my breath and pull out my phone, only to curse louder when I see Antony's name on my screen. Gio must have given him my number because I know I sure the fuck didn't.

"What?" I snap into the phone.

"You hired my DAUGHTER!" Antony's angry voice comes over the line.

I almost kissed your daughter. I wisely keep that retort in my head. The last thing I need is to put a match to that powder keg.

"Someone needed to! You weren't helping her! She has been drowning for THREE YEARS, and you couldn't be bothered to get off your ass and care for her!" I slash a frustrated hand through the air, and the portafilter flies across the room. I rub the bridge of my nose. Today is not going as planned.

"She knew what going to the States meant. She is the one who decided that was what she wanted—"

I cut him off. "She has been working two jobs to afford FOOD, you pretentious bastard! Tough parenting is one thing, and then there's neglect.

And here's a hint, boyo. You are so firmly in the neglect category it should be reported."

Antony snorts. "You can't neglect an adult child. She made her own choices and gets to live with them. You had no right to stick your nose where it doesn't belong."

"Maybe so, Antony, but you know what? I bet all those posh friends of yours would think differently if they knew how you've been treating Maisie. I mean, the poor girl who lost her mother and got shipped off to a man she barely knew, then shoved into a boarding school and forgotten, only to graduate and have to work two jobs to afford a cup of noodles? That's not a good look when her father is worth millions, now is it? All it would take is a word to the wrong group." I *tsk* my tongue, like I'm ashamed of him. And I am. My opinion doesn't mean shit, though. But his social circle? Oh, they matter.

"You wouldn't dare..." Antony seethes, and I hear a voice screeching in the background. A voice I never want to hear again. Monica. I roll my eyes at their antics. Some things never change. Antony could never accept accountability at uni either.

"Now listen to me, MATE." My voice is dark and deadly. I'm done with this jackass. "You will start to support your daughter the way she deserves, AS YOUR DAUGHTER, or I will. Your choice. Make it soon. Either way, she will have a job here for as long as she wants it."

I hang up the phone and chuck it onto my desk in frustration. I take a minute to breathe and calm down. Turning around, I see the mess of my espresso machine again and chuckle. I clean up the scattered grounds and put the machine back together. Thankfully, nothing's broken. It was just in the wrong spots.

Truth is, I wouldn't have cared if she broke the machine. I can buy a hundred of the same models and never break a sweat. It was the thought behind what she tried to do that I couldn't replace. How long has it been since someone cared enough to do such a small thing for me like make me a coffee without a hidden agenda?

I stare at the wooden door to my office as if I can see her, and the smell of coffee fills the space. Grabbing my cup, I move around and sit back in my chair. The pile of projects I requested is placed neatly on top of my desk with the notes typed up and paper clipped to each folder. The assistant position is below where she could be in my company. Still, it gives her the ability to focus on other aspects as well as earn a living.

Pushing the files aside, I draft an email to the private investigator I keep on retainer. Time to learn a bit more about Miss Mitchell.

Chapter 9

Maisie

I rush out to my desk on wobbly knees. Jack almost kissed me. ME! *Maisie Mitchell!*

I sink into my chair, pressing my trembling fingers on my lips. He would have kissed me, but Father called. What could he possibly want with Jack? According to Uncle Gio, they haven't spoken in years.

Could it be a coincidence that I started working here, and Father calls for the first time in over five years?

I grab my purse from my desk. I need to take a break and be anywhere but here. I can't do this right now. I dash for the lift, only to have Stella intercept me before I can press the button.

"Whoa, Maisie, are you okay? You're running like the hounds of hell are after you! Did you get in trouble?" She pulls me closer and lowers her voice. "You didn't get fired for standing up for me, did you?"

"No. No. It's nothing like that, but I have to go. I've-I've..." I'm looking around, trying to figure out exactly what I have to do.

"Okay. Let's go get a coffee, huh? Doesn't that sound nice?" Stella grabs me by the hand and pushes the button to guide me to the canteen.

We each select a coffee and a muffin from the machine, and she pulls me over to a table in a quiet corner.

"Okay. Talk," she says.

So I do. I tell her everything. From growing up with my mum in Sydney to the accident that claimed her life, to finding out who my father was, and then moving in with him and my stepmum. I tell Stella about how he refused to let me stay with my nan, stuck me in a posh boarding school in London, and ignored me even when I graduated.

I share how he wanted me to go to Oxford, but I wanted to choose my own path and opted to attend school in the States despite the cost. I even tell her I spent the last three years working two jobs while attending classes. By the time I wrap up my story, the muffins are nothing but crumbs, and what little coffee we have left is cold.

"Well." Stella clears her throat. "What a colossal ass!"

A small chuckle escapes my lips. A part of me feels bad, because he's *my father*. "You're not wrong. It just happened to work out that Uncle Gio knew Mr. Foster needed an assistant and arranged my interview." I stare into my cup, so I don't see Stella's jaw drop but I do hear the sudden hitch in her voice.

"Your Uncle *Gio*?"

"Um, yeah. Why?"

"What's his last name?"

"Santoro?"

"OH-MY-GOD!"

"What?"

Stella shoves her chair back before standing and pointing at me. "GIO SANTORO IS YOUR UNCLE!"

I look around nervously. Lucky for me, the few employees in the canteen appear to ignore Stella's outburst. "I mean, he's not really my uncle. He went to school with my dad and Jack—Mr. Foster. So, when we met, he told me to call him Uncle Gio. He's always been really kind to me." I tug on my hair.

"Okay. So, let's break this down. You needed a job that would allow you to finish your internship hours and still live. Your Uncle *Gio Santoro* pulled some strings, and you were hired here. However, you are more than qualified for the position. So, what's the issue?"

"Father called Mr. Foster. Uncle Gio said they haven't spoken in a decade or more. It can't be a coincidence that the first time they talk is also my first day working here."

Stella bites her lip. "No. It can't be, but you don't know what they're talking about. It could be—" Her words are cut off by a chime from my phone.

Picking it up, I see two text messages. The one from my bank says I received a deposit of $25,000. The second text is from Father telling me to ask Jack to do things I will never repeat and not to expect him to send me any more money when this is gone.

I set my phone back down and cross my arms over my chest. "Well, I think I understand what was said. I have to talk to Mr. Foster about minding his business and staying out of my family drama."

Stella drinks the last of her cold coffee before pushing to her feet. "Oh, boy. Here we go."

I barge into Mr. Foster's office, and he stares at me wide-eyed before hanging up the phone. "What did you tell Father?" I'm so angry I'm practically vibrating.

"Excuse me?"

"What. Did. You. Tell. Father?" I approach his desk, gripping the edge so hard my knuckles are white.

"The truth, Maisie. I told him the truth about his actions and how they would be perceived. About how what he is doing is child abuse—to his own daughter, no less—and that if the word got out to his social circle, he might find a different reaction. I'm guessing he reached out to you then?"

I never considered myself a violent person, but Jack's calm, rational tone makes me want to throw things directly at his head. "You had no right! None! The last thing I want *or need* is his hush money! I was doing just fine on my own!" I toss my unlocked phone onto the desk in front of him.

Jack picks it up and views the one-sided text thread with Father, since the man hardly ever replies to me. "How much did he send you?"

"Why does it matter! It's money I don't want!"

"But you need it, Maisie! I know you want to stand on your own, but helping provide for you is the bare minimum he should be doing as your parent! He has literal millions. Did you know that? Millions! He should support you no matter where you want to study! So, take the money, pay off what you need to pay off, and do something fun with the rest. Update your wardrobe, go out to eat, see a play—well, I'll give you my seats at the opera if you want." Jack stands and comes around the desk, stopping in front of me. "I don't want you to just keep on existing. I want you to LIVE." Jack reaches out and cups my cheek again.

I feel the tears pooling in my eyes because every word is almost a physical punch to the gut. How long have I just been *existing*? Trying to make it from one day to the next? How long has it been since I was just able to be carefree and happy? The fact that Jack can see all of that after only knowing me one day makes my heart ache.

Since I went against Father's wishes and he cut me off, I've only existed, trying to make it from shift to shift, job to job. While Father would probably consider the amount an insult—a pittance—for me, it's life-changing.

"How did you know?" My voice catches in my throat, which has suddenly become too tight.

"Because, my darling, once upon a time, we weren't that different. I see you, Maisie, and if I can do something to ease your burden, I will. Go home. I'll see you tomorrow." Jack's hand drops from my face, and he walks around his chair. Without a doubt, I've been dismissed.

I walk back to my desk, where Stella is waiting while chewing on her thumbnail. When I grab my bag from where I flung it in my earlier snit, she grabs my shoulders and shakes me. "Did you get fired? I couldn't hear a thing. What did he say? What did *you* say? What did he do? What did *you* do?" Her voice ends on a wail, and I grab her arms to get her to stop shaking me.

"He told me to take the rest of the day off. He said I should use the money to pay off my school debt and maybe update my wardrobe. Where would I go for that?"

Stella grins like a kid in a candy store. "Fifth Avenue, of course! Let's go! I know all the best shops! Let's update that wardrobe!" She hooks her arm in mine and drags me toward the lift.

"Stella! You have work!"

"I'll finish it tomorrow. This is a once-in-a-lifetime, rom-com, *Pretty Woman* moment, and I will not miss it! To the shops!" The lift door closes on her war cry, and I can't help but shake my head.

What have I done?

Chapter 10

Jack

It's 6:15 in the morning, a week after Maisie started working for me. My calendar is now balanced, projects are on the right track toward completion, and I could swear that our efficiency has doubled since I decided to hire Maisie Mitchell. I even find myself smiling more.

Her soft voice is constant in the background, and I leave my door open just to hear her. I've just sipped my coffee when Maisie walks into my office. No, she doesn't walk. She saunters. It seems she's taken my advice to heart. Gone are the demure skirts and black flats, and in their place, the silk button-up paired with black pencil skirts that cling to every curve, and at least six-inch heels. I swallow my coffee, hoping it will remove my tongue from the roof of my mouth. I'm still staring when she stops in front of my desk and looks up from her clipboard.

"What?"

"Nothing. I'm sorry. Let's go over the calendar." I set my cup down and straightened my tie.

Maisie gives me a skeptical look but returns her focus to her clipboard. "Okay. Well, you have a 9 a.m. meeting with Eaton, a 10 a.m. with accounting, and a noon lunch at Julianie's. There's no agenda posted. We've moved the project meetings from yesterday to today at 4 p.m. Here are the projection reports, HR reports, and a note from—to be honest, I'm not sure who. But it's on... *this*." Maisie gingerly passes me a napkin, her pert nose wrinkled in disgust. "I pray that it's tomato sauce."

"Ah." I take the napkin. "That would be from Eaton, my CFO. He's brilliant but scatterbrained, so he habitually grabs whatever he can find when he has an idea, question, or something he needs to do. He remembers to write it down at least, on whatever's available unfortunately. It would be remiss of me to say this is my first napkin note, and I doubt it will be the last. To answer your question, yes, that is ketchup."

Maisie wrinkles her nose again before returning to her desk, and I open my emails to find one from my PI. It seems the preliminary check I ran on Maisie matches everything Gio told me about her before the interview. What I don't expect is the note attached at the end.

Antony's family knew about Maisie and paid her mother to stay away. Family friends of her mother stated that Maisie never knew about the money or who her father may have been until the DNA testing had been done. Maisie and her mother had lived a modest life in a little beach town near Sydney, where her grandmother still lives in a retirement community. The woman is in the beginning stages of Alzheimer's, which explains why Maisie is intent to return to Australia after her degree.

I sit here staring at the report, repeatedly reviewing it and sorting out the implications. While this has no bearing on Maisie and her job with me, I debate telling her what the PI discovered, unsure if she'll even want to know.

Would she be upset or angry that I hired a PI? Would she want to see that she could have had a different, more privileged life all these years? I can't see how the knowledge would benefit her now.

I'm still staring at my screen when a knock on my door has me looking up, and Eaton walks in. "I thought we were meeting at nine?" I grab my notepad from my desk, trying to look busy.

"It's 9:05. Are you okay?" Eaton slides into a chair and crosses his feet at the ankle.

"Sorry. I got caught up with something and lost track of time." I make quick notes, flip the page, and pick up the napkin. "You wanted to talk about—" I squint at his scribbling. "The IPA?"

"The IPO. I wanted to talk about the IPO. Right now, though, I want to talk about that sweet little thing you have admining for you. She's new. Can I have her when you're done?"

For some reason I don't want to look too closely at, I fight the sudden urge to knock my oldest business partner's smug smile straight off his face. I grip my pen and stare at him instead. "No. Hands off my assistant, you lecherous bastard. I won't have you doing anything that would make her uncomfortable. You know the rules."

Eaton grins and pushes his blonde hair out of his face while adjusting his glasses. At six-foot-four, he's built. We frequent the gym together. But where I tend to be darker and more somber, he gives off more of a pretty boy surfer mixed with nerd vibe. This fact plays up in his favor every spring break. I've never minded his good looks before now, and we've been known to be each other's wingmen.

"Anyway. The reason I wanted to chat was about the IPO."

"What about it? You said that it was all wrapped up and ready to go."

"It was supposed to be. But several projects are overdue, which delays the financial review."

"Yes. I know. Shit. I have a stack of files I need to sift through. We had to fire the lead analyst." I grab the folders and spread them out on my desk.

"Ah. Yeah. Lucy, the man-eater, or so I hear. She really made the rounds."

"What does that mean?"

"You can't be that obtuse. She, ah, slept around. If the scuttlebutt is true, it's how she got to lead several important projects. There was one manager... I can't think of his name at the moment, but they were hot and heavy for a while despite his wife and three kids. I don't usually listen to idle office gossip, but the rumor's been around for a while, and I've seen some things that make me believe it's true."

By the end of his spiel, my jaw has hit my desk. "How could you possibly know all this?"

What has been going on in my business?

"Analysts! They know everything, and they're a bunch of horrible gossips! You should go down to the canteen sometimes. Well, maybe not you. Everyone would recognize you, and the tea would dry up." Eaton pushes his glasses up his nose again, a surefire sign he's excited.

"Get out of my office. I have work to do."

Eaton grins and straightens up from his chair.

Before he reaches the other side of the room, I call out, "Can we try to limit the napkin notes?" I wave the flimsy material at him, and he chuckles before he opens the door to leave.

"Maisie, my lovely! How are you today? I wanted to ask..." he says but he shuts the door on the rest of his statement.

I stand from my desk, stride over, and wrench it open again. I see Eaton leaning casually against Maisie's desk while she smiles up at him. "Eaton! Don't you have somewhere to be?"

He laughs before winking at Maisie and strolling toward the elevator.

"That was rude." Maisie laughs.

"He wet the bed until he was ten," I grumble.

"Oh, well. That's good to know. So, you've known each other a long time, then?"

"You could say that. We had very similar upbringings that led to us crossing paths over the years. While I attended Oxford, he went to school here in the States."

Maisie grimaces at the mention of uni, but I continue speaking anyway.

"When I decided to start my company, I knew there was no one else I would want to go into business with. Eaton graduated at the top of his class and was already making waves in the business world. He's truly brilliant. A little crazy but brilliant. He convinced me to move the company here, and the rest is history."

"It must be nice to have a friend like that in your life. Someone you can count on." Maisie answers the phone, and I hear the shrieking from where I stand. "Ma'am. Ma'am. Please, ma'am, I—" she says.

I reach out, pry the phone from her hand, and hang it up. "You never, ever have to put up with this. Ever."

Maisie laughs, and I find myself smiling in return. Her joy is infectious. Except during my dressing down for speaking out of turn to Antony, I don't think I've ever seen her anything but happy. It's refreshing. I look at her closely. Her hair is curled around her shoulders and back. She looks rested, and signs of a sack lunch disappeared after the first day. I find myself inordinately pleased with the fact that she's thriving here.

Maisie lifts a challenging brow. "Maybe you should be more careful who you date because that was Regina."

I grimace. "Still?"

"Still," she repeats.

"Don't worry. I'll handle it." I head back to my office and shut my door. Maisie doesn't need to hear what is about to happen. So far, she's only known Jack Foster, a friend of her uncle and a pretty easygoing boss. But I've heard the rumors, and they're true. She doesn't need to meet Jack Frost, the man about to set a few things straight with a former lover who's overstepping.

Chapter 11

Maisie

My days at Foster Inc are peaceful, and I enjoy it. For two months, I've worked long hours, but they are broken up by lunch with Stella, who was assigned as team lead on several new projects and recently seems to have caught the eye of one Eaton Masters, CFO.

That's where we are right now. Enjoying a quiet lunch. At least we were... until Stella decides to drop a bomb on me. "When will you admit that Jack Frost wants you to thaw his frozen heart?"

I nearly choke on my chips. "Stella! He wants no such thing!" I can feel my face heating as a blush streams across my cheeks. *Curse my pale skin.*

"Puh-lease. Everyone knows it but you, girl. He stares at you like you're his favorite meal, and he's on death row. You joke and banter. And I swear I heard him laughing when you told him that joke about the kangaroo and the dingo the other day. I've been working here for four years and never even knew the man could smile. His door was never open. He only took an interest in the company's bottom line. Since you started, his door is always open, he's upgraded the canteen with your favorite foods, and he's approved a more generous holiday package because you once spent forty-five minutes going on about everything you love about Christmas. You both constantly prank each other—girl, he buys you whatever you request for the office."

"Stella. You're nuts. I'm leaving in a month. We've just spent a lot of time together and developed a friendship. That's all."

"Mhmmm. I have some oceanfront property in Arizona to sell you if you believe a single thing that's come out of your own mouth, Maisie Mitchell."

"You're crazy." I clear my tray before making my way to the lift.

I then head straight to my desk when the doors open on my floor. I stop at the threshold to Jack's office and watch him read over a report for a moment. It is a Friday afternoon, so the schedule has a lot of downtime. Jack prefers it this way because it sets the tone for a relaxing weekend. Stella's comment about him giving me whatever I want floats in my head, and I suddenly want to test the theory. I know Jack loathes my favorite holiday. What I don't know is why. So I challenge myself to find out.

"I have an idea!"

Jack's head pops up, and for a split second, I see what I think is hunger in his gaze before he carefully blanks his face. "Miss Mitchell has an idea. I'm officially quaking in my Oxfords. What is this idea, then?" His tone is teasing, which completely contradicts how he usually reacts.

"I want to get a head start on decorating the office for Christmas. I don't want to leave it for the last minute since I won't be here much longer."

Jack frowns, leaving me to wonder which statement is giving him pause. "Of course. Decorate the outer office and the rest of the building as you see fit. I'll give you the number of the company we usually use. You can plan the Christmas party too, if you want."

I watch as he opens an email, presumably sending me the information he mentioned, and squeak out a brisk "okay" before I return to my desk. Where I grab my phone and text Stella.

Me: I'm planning the company Christmas party, and he gave me permission to decorate the office.

I chew on my thumbnail as the dots dance at the bottom of the screen.

Stella: I knew it! Sorry... I ducked into the ladies to avoid Eaton. Anyway, so it's true. The pretty Aussie thawed Jack Frost's heart after all!

Me: It isn't like that, and you know it!

Stella: He hasn't been as grumpy since you started. I know he watches you like he's afraid you'll disappear. I also know that in all my time here, we never had a company Christmas party, nor has the office been decorated for the holiday.

I can almost hear her gloating. Rolling my eyes, I write a quick text back.

Me: Just for that, you're helping me plan this.

Stella: Jeez. Fine. Uh-oh, I can hear Eaton calling my name. GTG.

I drop my phone back into my purse and open my inbox. Jack's email stares back at me. I want to click on it, but a more pressing subject line catches my attention. Marcus McIntyre canceling his appointment.

Oh boy, this will not go over well at all.

I make a quick phone call before getting up and walking over to Jack's open door. "So. Mr. Foster? I just got an email…" I trail off.

"Well, Miss Mitchell, you receive many emails at your job. What makes this one noteworthy?"

I clear my throat. "It's from Marcus McIntyre. He's canceling his meeting with you."

Jack sets down the report he is reading and removes his glasses, which gives him more of a devil-may-care vibe—sexier than I am prepared to admit.

"Did he say why?" While his tone is civil, I feel the chill coating the words. Mr. Foster is gone, Jack Frost firmly in his stead.

I shift nervously. "He did not. I called his assistant, who said he was preparing for a trip to Aspen with his family. I managed to get the dates from her, but she wouldn't give me more information than that." I place the notes on his desk and take a few steps back.

"Miss Mitchell, please go to the canteen and have a break. Maybe Miss Jarvis will want to join you. I'll text you when you can come back up. Oh, if you happen to come across Eaton on your way down, please ask him to stop by my office. That will be all."

I grab my purse and quickly swing by Stella's workspace.

"What's the hurry? Is the building on fire?" She barely has time to swipe up her phone before I'm dragging her away from her desk.

"I got an email from Marcus McIntyre's assistant canceling the meeting."

"No! Why?"

"I don't know. All I do know is that Marcus is going to be in Aspen next week. Even that took some sweet talking to pry out of his assistant. When I told Mr. Foster, he got super quiet and asked me to take a break and tell Eaton to come to his office if I saw him."

"What!" Stella begins to type on her phone.

"What are you doing?" I try to peek over her shoulder.

"Texting Eaton to go see Mr. Foster." Her fingers fly over the keys, but the screen is tilted so I can't read it.

"Eaton, huh?" I stand on my tiptoes, trying to read the message chain while hating being short.

Stella blushes. "That's not important. What *is* important is finding out why McIntyre canceled the meeting on such short notice..."

"We'll come back to that. As far as the meeting goes, I don't know. It doesn't make sense." By this time, our lattes are ready, so we grab them and a couple of muffins. "I worked up that portfolio myself. It's a mutually beneficial arrangement for all parties. There is nothing hinky or even remotely one-sided with the contract."

"When do you leave again? Also, I can't believe you're leaving! The office won't be the same without you. I swear you've turned this company around in such a short time. I will miss you!"

"I officially have a month left. However, I've *unofficially* been approved to return to Australia before Christmas to be with my nan. I haven't been home for more than high school breaks since I left when my mother passed. I only got to go on those because Father didn't want me at the house. To be fair, I didn't want to be there either so it worked for us. I'm more than ready to see her again." I smile at the thought of my nan.

"Well, I really will miss you. You have to promise to keep in touch."

"I promise." I clasp hands with Stella across the table. My phone chirps, and I look down. "I've been summoned back upstairs. Guess our break is over."

Stella and I exit the elevator and split off in opposite directions. I head toward Jack's office and stumble across Eaton as he's leaving.

"Ah. Miss Mitchell. Welcome back. Enjoy your little break?" His megawatt smile does nothing for me and only irritates Jack, who's presently standing behind him.

"Stop flirting with my assistant and work on what we discussed." Eaton winks at me as he strolls to the lift..

"Come with me, please, Miss Mitchell." Jack returns to his office, and I grab my steno pad and follow him. "I want you to book a cabin in Aspen for two weeks. I want you to schedule a meeting with Marcus at his earliest convenience. I also need all the prep files and any possible research brought to Aspen. I don't want to lose this contract because of our negligence. Call my valet and have him pack my bags. Make sure you pack warmly—if you require additional winter wear, please call Saks and have it charged to my account."

My pen stutters across the page. "Additional winter wear? Why would I need additional winter wear for you to go to Aspen?"

"Because you are going too." His tone suggests the answer should be obvious.

"What do you mean *I'm going too*?"

"Miss Mitchell, you have been an integral part of this endeavor. For you to not be there, should something arise, would be nothing short of gross negligence of the highest order. Now, pack your bags. We're going to Aspen."

Chapter 12

Jack

I look around the tiny cabin and want to turn around and walk out. We are miles from the main resort, and the owner of this particular cabin is obsessed with everything Christmas—if the decorations are any indication. A fully adorned Christmas tree stands proudly next to a cheery fireplace below the wooden mantle with two stockings. Garland and ribbons festoon the banister to the second floor, where the bedrooms are, while glass nativities and Christmas villages rest upon almost every flat surface.

"Miss Mitchell. Is this payback for asking you to accompany me on this trip?" I flick a dismissive finger against a nearby snowman.

Maisie trudges behind me, covered head to toe in winter wear that is more appropriate for Antarctica than Colorado. She hangs her parka on a peg by the door before grabbing her satchel and slamming it angrily on the bar.

"No. This is all that was available at the last minute for the time you requested this close to the holidays. Why? What's wrong with it?" Her harsh tone melts away when she sees the great room. "Oh, how lovely! They even put up a tree for us! That is so sweet."

She flits about the space, admiring every piece of Christmas tchotchkes she comes across. I drop both suitcases and groan.

How can she honestly enjoy all this... this cheer?

"If we could get back to the business at hand?" I know my tone is short when Maisie glares at me a little before grabbing her satchel and pulling out her steno pad.

The second week she was with me, I bought her an iPad for notes. As far as I know, it's still in the box at the bottom of a drawer in her desk. However, I have seen her go through at least thirty steno pads meticulously arranged by date.

She flings herself into a nearby chair, crosses her legs, and looks at me pointedly before flipping open her notes. "Marcus agreed to a meeting tomorrow, at noon, at Element 47, followed by drinks, if required. He is available only once if you want to meet him to ski for the next three days. Apparently, he's scheduled events with his family and will not be available again until the very end of our trip. He will attend the meeting as long as it includes hot chocolate—his words, not mine—although I agree. And for the record, you will not be getting me on skis ever." Maisie closes the steno pad a tad aggressively. "Thank you very much." She stalks over to the table to pull files from the banker boxes we had couriered over from the private airstrip.

"How am I expected to meet at Element 47 when we're staying this far from The Little Nell?" I know my words are clipped, and Maisie doesn't deserve it. Still, I'm finding my control slipping around my little assistant.

Maisie glares at me over her shoulder. "We will have to ride the snowmobiles parked outside. Like I told you, this was the only cabin with an open booking this far into the season. It was this cabin or no cabin. And no cabin wasn't an option, so here we are in this frozen hellscape. I would also like to add if you think you are getting me on one of those death machines, you are sadly mistaken. I will not be stepping out into that frozen wasteland any more than I have to."

I shake my head at her antics before swiping up both suitcases and taking them upstairs. After a quick peek in the bedrooms, I deposit Maisie's in the one with the best view. It may be a small consolation, but it's all I can give her right now.

I walk into the bathroom to find even more festive Christmas junk. Gathering it all up in my arms, I dump everything in the one recliner in the room before hopping in the shower. A delicious smell wafts upstairs when I finally open the stall door again. I take my time getting dressed before returning downstairs.

On a good day, Maisie doesn't hold a grudge, but today is a bad day, as she's obviously irritated with me. Dragging her out here to Colorado has put me firmly in her bad books, and I'm desperately trying to give her time to calm down. That said, after the little incident in the living room, I can only imagine her irritation has kicked up a notch.

I make my way to the kitchen and am floored by the vision in front of me. Maisie is dancing around, her long blonde hair pulled up into a messy bun on her head, while she sings Christmas carols at the top of her lungs. At the same time, something simmers on the stove, giving off the most fantastic aroma.

But what stops me dead in my tracks is the sight of Maisie's ass in a pair of tight black leggings, her chest accentuated by a fitted tank top. I've seen women of all walks of life wear this type of workout wear and never had an issue, but on Maisie, it's downright sinful.

I watch her maneuver around the kitchen, wholly comfortable and oblivious to my presence, and she radiates happiness. I think back on all the changes in my office since she arrived. Productivity is up, we've landed several new contracts, and employee satisfaction is high. The halls are now filled with laughter and chatter as people work far more productively. The place is not the silent tomb it was before.

She's happy. It hits me with an almost physical force, strong enough to bring me to my knees.

The song changes to something with a deeper, more suggestive beat. When Maisie's dancing switches to match, I decide that I'm really not a masochist and clear my throat, only to have a wooden spoon smack me in the face.

Chapter 13

Maisie

I watch in horror as the sauce-covered spoon slides off Jack's face and onto the floor. Flecks of sauce decorate his cream-colored sweater, which looks like it costs more than my monthly rent.

What is it made of? Baby alpaca wool?

I stand here, contemplating the composition of my boss's clothes for far too long. Until I realize we've been silently staring at each other and jump into action. "Oh, oh no. Give it to me, and I'll put it in cold water. We can save it. I can clean it. I can clean it." I tug ineffectually at the hem of Jack's sweater, trying to get it over his head while he tries to hold it down.

"Miss Mitchell." Jack pushes at my wrists as we grapple for the sweater. And for a moment, he appears to have the upper hand. However, after the utterly accidental discovery of his ticklish spots under his arms and, ironically, his elbows, I end up victorious.

Crowing triumphantly, I rush to the sink and shove the sweater under the cold water, swishing the sauce spots to try to loosen them. "It's okay. I can get the stains out. It's okay." I'm so focused on my task that I don't hear Jack calling my name from behind me until he forcefully grabs me by the shoulders and turns me around to face him.

"Maisie! I don't give a damn about the sweater! Calm down and listen."

Given the height difference, I'm face to face with his toned chest. A light sprinkling of hair dusts his pecs in a trail down to his jeans, hanging low on his hips. I swallow roughly before raising my eyes to meet his. Jack's jaw is clenched while his hands almost massage my shoulders. He presses me between his warm body and the sink.

On reflex, my palms come up and rest on his pecs. He pulls me closer, and the heat radiating off him is a jarring contrast to the cold water splashing up from the tap. He rubs his nose over my hair, breathing deeply, and I can feel the groan rattling in his chest.

"Jack." His name leaves my mouth in a whisper, but it still breaks the spell, and he jerks back, putting several feet between us. I clutch the benchtop behind me as we stare at each other for an eternity.

"Don't worry about the sweater. You can throw it away. I'm going to go get a new shirt." Jack turns abruptly and heads upstairs.

It takes several more minutes before I collect myself enough to turn off the tap and wring out the garment. Most of the splotches are pale pink by now, and after checking the tag, I'm sure I can get the rest out with a bit of elbow grease.

Setting the sweater aside, I grab a sponge and cleaner to wipe up the floor. Placing the kitchen to rights centers me, and I can think again when I'm done. I hang Jack's sweater over the drying rack in the laundry, spray on a bit of spot remover I found in a cabinet, and leave it to soak.

I'm spooning up the chili when Jack joins me in the kitchen again. I give him a tight smile and sit at the far end of the table with my own sleeve of crackers. Jack grabs sour cream and shredded cheese out of the fridge.

I shake my head. *Of course, he would go all out.*

"The fridge is well stocked. Did you arrange that?" Jack grabs a bottle of Pelligrino before taking his seat.

I nod and finish chewing my food. "I provided a list of groceries I got from your housekeeper, added a few of my own, and paid the owners an extra fee to have the place stocked. Apparently, this cabin isn't booked often due to its distance from the resort, so the hosts were thrilled we were interested. Jocelyn, the wife, was so grateful she made us several meals and left them for us to reheat. Hence the chili."

We eat in silence before we both decide to break it at the same time.

"Look—"

"Jack—"

Jack chuckles as we each stumble over what to say. "I was very unprofessional earlier. I want to apologize. I never want you to feel anything other than comfortable here with me."

I wave him off. "No, no. I know it was a… mishap. We're good. It's okay."

When we finish eating, and the continued silence grows to be too much, I clear my throat and grab one of the boxes we brought.

"So, let's go over the plan for tomorrow. Here's what we know." I pull the file close to me. "Marcus McIntyre is married with two kids, Maxim and Calista, twins, age seventeen. His wife, Alexandra, is his business partner and works in their marketing department. According to his secretary, Marcus is a family man, golfs on weekends, attends his kids' sporting events, school functions, and so on." I peer up from my notes. "I don't see anything indicating why he would pull the contract. I assisted with the terms, which appear very beneficial for both parties. You'd both stand to make a large sum." I push up from the table to place our dishes in the sink and flip the switch on the kettle.

"I tapped all my known sources, and no one's heard anything. We'll likely find out tomorrow." Jack's frustration is evident in his tone and crossed arms.

I shrug, pull some mugs down from the cabinet, and grab the hot chocolate packets from the pantry. "It may have nothing to do with the terms at all."

"What do you mean?"

"Well, we can agree that the contract is solid. Both companies stand to gain profits and market shares. There's no logical reason for Marcus not to sign, so maybe his reasoning isn't logical." I dump the packets into the cups, adding boiling water to each.

"Continue."

"Well, it could have to do with something that happened to him when he interacted with someone from your company." I grab the can of squirty cream from the fridge, adding a generous serving to my mug and an average amount to Jack's.

"What the hell does that mean?"

"Well, for example. If I were out to dinner and saw someone misbehaving at the bar... They're loud, swearing, pushing, and generally causing a ruckus, which then forces the manager to come over and escort them out. And I notice they're wearing a company shirt—let's say for a lawn service—I know that I would think twice about hiring that company to mow my lawn based on how that one employee was behaving. The employee will probably get fired, and it isn't the company's fault that one employee acted out of turn on his own time. However, my opinion of that company is now tarnished. Maybe something similar happened with him and someone in your circle?" I set the mugs on the table before reclaiming my seat.

Jack stares at me. So I grab a napkin and wipe my chin, thinking I may have some cream on it. When it comes back clean, I shift nervously in my chair until I can't take it anymore.

"What?"

"You're a genius." Jack continues to stare at me in awe.

"What are you on about?"

"You're a genius. I never would have thought about something like that. I never would have made the connection, never would have connected those dots. You're absolutely brilliant. What am I going to do when you leave?"

"You'll be okay. I'm sure you'll find someone even more amazing than me." I blush at his compliments. "Even if I stayed, I couldn't be your assistant. I've worked too hard to get past this part of my life. I appreciate the help with the internship hours and the job. I can never thank you enough, but this is not where I'm meant to be."

"No, I don't think it is, Maisie," Jack murmurs. "I'm going to head to bed. We have to be ready to leave by eight tomorrow. I purchased dining privileges, so we need to check in for our entrance cards. They're linked to the company account, so anything you charge is covered."

"Sounds good. I'll be ready. I'll finish up down here and then head to bed as well. Sweet dreams, Jack."

"Sweet dreams, Maisie." Jack's voice floats back into the room as he ascends the stairs.

I clean the kitchen and remove the sauce stains from the sweater as best I can, quickly washing it by hand before laying it back over the drying rack for the night. Then I take a quick shower and slip into my favorite flannel pajamas. By the time my head hits the pillow, I'm already out.

Chapter 14

Jack

Listening to Maisie shower is a form of torture I never expected to experience. My mind keeps envisioning her pressed up against me again. I could feel the brush of her breasts on my chest with her every breath. I'll never forget the way her eyes dilated while she stared up at me in shock. Every instinct I have is demanding that I walk into that bedroom and claim her. It's a pounding, incessant thought marching in my brain.

I grip the sheets tightly as the shower turns off and imagine her stepping out onto the mat, wrapping the bath towel around her wet body with her hair in another messy bun on the top of her head.

Maisie moves around in her room for a few more minutes before the house quiets. I slowly relax my grip on the sheets, rolling over and staring at the empty space next to me in my bed, wondering what she would look like laid out there, her eyes closed while her white-blonde hair drapes over the dark sheets.

I close my eyes and try to think about anything else to dispel the image. Memories of Antony and Monica in bed together rise to the surface, and I grit my teeth as my body finally calms.

Right. Business. We're here for business and nothing more. I must keep my eye on the prize and my hands off Miss Maisie Mitchell. Rolling back over, I pound my pillow and fall into my worst sleep in years.

***

I wake up the following day and force myself to sit on the side of the bed, rubbing my face in exhaustion. I need to get moving, be on my A-game, and close this deal. However, as I focus on regaining my lost motivation, the familiar sounds and smells from the kitchen seep into my consciousness, offering a comforting respite from my fatigue.

Throwing on a sweater, I pad downstairs, my socks soundless on the steps. When I reach the living room area that opens to the kitchen, I can see Maisie tossing something repeatedly in a skillet. Whatever she's cooking smells divine, and my stomach grumbles in appreciation. Maisie dances around again, singing and cooking, completely oblivious to my approach.

"Good Morning." I smile wide when she once again squeaks and jumps in surprise. This time, I'm out of the danger zone, and my sweater remains safe.

"*You. Need. A. BELL!*" Maisie seethes playfully while aiming the kitchen utensil in my direction. She glares at me before turning around and grabbing something. Then she slams it down in front of me. An Americano.

I pick up the cup and take a sip. It's perfect, as always. "What are you cooking? It smells delicious." I lean over to see all the different pots and pans on the stove.

"I'm making a fry-up." She's slicing, dicing, and flipping things, and I watch in wonder as a full plate sits in front of me a few minutes later. There are eggs, bacon, mushrooms, and some beans.

"Are those baked beans?" I poke at the offending legume.

"Well, it wouldn't be a proper fry-up without them, now would it?" Maisie grabs her own plate and heads for the table.

I follow suit. "I wouldn't know, seeing as I've never had one." I pick up a piece of toast and take a bite. It's perfectly buttered.

"How did you live with Gio and my dad all those years and never have a fry-up?" She spears a mushroom, humming to herself as she chews.

"College boys are not always the best at cooking. I think we mostly lived on dodgy kebabs and ramen." I try the mushrooms and groan at how delicious they are. Suddenly starving, I attack everything else on the plate. I can't help but marvel at how tasty it all is—somehow it works together too.

"That makes sense. Once we're done, I'll need about twenty minutes to get ready. I have the files prepared." Maisie sips her coffee and taps the case in the middle of the table. "It's a laptop bag, so it's waterproof, since we have to travel by snowmobile."

"That's a good idea. It shouldn't take me long to get ready either. This breakfast is amazing, Miss Mitchell. Thank you! I didn't expect you to cook on this trip, but I am glad you are."

"I don't mind. Cooking has always been something I enjoy. It reminds me of spending time in the kitchen with my mum and Nan. They are some of the happiest memories of my life." She smiles while she says it, but the gesture is tinged with sadness.

"I'm sorry to hear about your mom. I never met her, but she must have been an amazing person to raise someone like you."

Maisie's eyes tear up as she offers me a slight nod. "Yeah. Mum was the best. It wasn't easy getting pregnant at sixteen, but she always said she wouldn't have changed a single thing because she got the best kid in the world." Maisie wipes her eyes with her napkin before taking her plate to the sink. "I'm going to go get ready. I'll meet you in the living room in twenty."

I quickly load the dishwasher before heading upstairs myself. I'm back and waiting in the living room when I see Maisie. And burst out laughing. She's wearing an oversized puffy parka and three layers of pants. Which means she can barely navigate the steps.

"What in the world?" I'm still laughing when she finally makes it to the landing.

Maisie glares at me through the small opening in her clothing, enunciating her words with a vengeance. *"Snow. Is. A. NO."*

"Can you even get on the snowmobile? I think you have a few too many layers. Come here." I remove a few overcoats and one parka, and I'm left with a much more mobile and visible assistant. "It's not a far drive. You can squish up behind me. That way, my body will block most of the wind." I wrap her scarf back around her and tie it in place.

"Fine. Let's go. I hope the resort has hot chocolate. I'll need something after the hell that is today."

Listening to my assistant grumble is one of the most peculiar turn of events. It makes me grin in perverse pleasure, knowing that there is something that can break the eternal sunshine named Maisie Mitchell.

I trudge through the snow to the garage, entering the code to open the door before cranking up the machine. Letting it warm up before pulling it out of the structure. I again enter the code to close the door before returning to the front door to get Maisie.

"Let's get you on here." I help her straddle the machine before positioning myself in front of her. "Snug in close to me so I can help block some of the wind."

I grab her arms and tug them tight around my waist. Maisie presses herself flush against my back, and with the files tucked safely between us, off we go. It takes a half hour to reach the resort. The trails are tightly packed, and the ride is smooth. However, it does not ease Maisie's anxiety, and she stays pressed up against me the whole ride. She wobbles when we disembark and quickly rushes into the lobby with the giant fireplace. I chuckle and hook the snowmobile to the block warmer before following her inside.

I check us in at the front desk and grab our day passes for the week before helping Maisie shuck off all her outerwear. When she finally looks like herself again, I gape at her deep-burgundy sweater and woolen leggings that encase legs—which, despite her small stature, seem to go on for miles. She has on knee-length black leather boots and appears to be both casual and professional at the same time.

Maisie shakes out her hair before gathering close to the fire once more. "How can people think a place like this is fun? I'm a block of ice!"

I chuckle, and she glares at me. "C'mon. I'll buy you a hot chocolate, and we can add something stronger if you wish."

Maisie eagerly follows me to the dining area, and I place her at a table near the grand fireplace. I give our order to one of the servers and sit and watch as Maisie attempts to warm herself up.

"Are you going to make it?"

It's clear my amusement aggravates her as she continues to narrow her eyes at me. "I'll be fine. I just have to adjust. I'm not used to this weather and, frankly, I don't want to be. I want to finish this meeting and return to Australia and Nan."

The waiter sets the hot chocolate in front of her, and Maisie picks it up, clutching the mug tightly for its warmth.

"Well then, by all means, let's get you home to your nan."

I reach for my own mug of coffee, and we sit in companionable silence until a familiar figure enters the room. I stand and meet Marcus in the doorway.

"Mr. McIntyre. I'm so pleased you agreed to meet. Please join us. I hope you won't be too warm this close to the fire. My companion is finding the cooler temperatures somewhat challenging." I keep my tone light and my smile wide as I hold out a hand for him to shake.

Marcus McIntyre accepts the gesture before striding over to Maisie, murmuring a greeting while urging her to remain seated. "Of course, I do not mind sitting this close to the fireplace. I wouldn't want such a lovely woman to be cold. It can take a while to adjust to the temperature differences here if you aren't used to them. Where are you from, if I may be so bold as to ask?"

I watch Maisie and Marcus chat back and forth about Australia and how Marcus's family vacations here every year. I've seen the same thing with Maisie over the last three months. She's charm personified. Once they're in her presence, seeing how anyone can do anything but what she wants is almost impossible. By the time the conversation comes back to me, Marcus is putty in her hands.

"I hate to interrupt, but I don't want to take any more of your time away from your family than necessary. Shall we discuss the contract?" I set the documentation onto the table and slide it toward Marcus.

"See, Mr. Foster, I like that about you. You respect family time for everyone. I heard stories... how you turned your nose up at the ideals that are the foundation of my company: marriage, family, and commitment to a purpose greater than yourself. That's the reason I rejected your offer in the first place." Marcus taps the folder with his index finger.

"Mr. McIntyre, I assure you I value all those things as well. I'm not sure what stories you've heard, but they couldn't be further from the truth!" I'm scrambling, trying to salvage this conversation.

"So, it's not true that you said you would never get married and have a family because they were an outdated and parochial way to live your life?" Marcus signals the waiter before ordering a Scotch.

"I don't remember saying those exact words." I'm stumbling now. "But I can assure you they're untrue because..."

"He's engaged to me," Maisie interrupts, and we both turn to her with our jaws dropped in shock.

Chapter 15

Maisie

Oh shit. Oh. *Shit*. Why did I open my big mouth?

Nan was always telling me I needed to think before I spoke. And I always laughed her off. Well, those chickens have come home to roost. Jack stares at me like I've grown two heads, while Mr. McIntyre glances thoughtfully between us. I quickly take another sip of my hot chocolate as the silence continues to blanket the table.

"Yes." Jack clears his throat loudly. "Maisie and I are engaged."

Mr. McIntyre looks pointedly at my hand. I follow his line of sight to my empty ring finger and offer him a tight smile. "I wanted to use my nan's ring. She raised me for most of my life and always said she would leave it to me. However, she's in Australia. We're heading back for Christmas, and I will get it from her then."

It's not really a lie. I've loved that ring since I was small. I stare at my finger, imagining it there, and I can feel the tears welling up. Jack tugs me close to his side, and I squeak at the unexpected contact. He kisses my head, and I try to act like this is normal.

"I haven't heard anything about your engagement. Not even a whisper in the society pages." Marcus appears to be watching us carefully.

"Maisie has been working for me for several months as she finishes her degree. I didn't want to subject her to unwanted scrutiny while she was doing so. We fully plan to have an official announcement after the holidays." Jack moves his arm around my shoulders and settles me firmly against him.

I smile and sip my hot chocolate, refusing to dig deeper into the hole I find myself in.

"Well, that changes things. Let's put this dull business away." Marcus takes the contract and tucks it into his briefcase. "Why don't you and your lovely fiancée join my family today? The boys and I plan to ski, but my wife wanted to check out the spa and shop. I'm sure Maisie would enjoy it as well."

Without missing a beat, Jack smiles and agrees. "I've already set up a charge account with the resort, even though we're staying in a more remote cabin. We wanted some alone time, so we rented a little spot about half an hour away. I'm sure Maisie would love a day of pampering." Jack kisses my head again, and I can't help the butterflies that take flight in my stomach.

We stand up and head back to the lobby, where a gorgeous redhead is waiting with two teens. She seems to fuss at the son while the daughter scrolls on her phone.

"Zan!" Marcus calls out, and the redhead turns and smiles in our direction. "Marcus! That was quick. I didn't think you'd be ready yet."

Marcus pulls her close for a kiss before turning to us. "I stumbled upon some happy news. We're among the first to know that Mr. Foster and the lovely Maisie are engaged!"

The woman, who I now know is his wife, Alexandra, jumps up and down. And I have to smile. It's contagious. "Well, that is happy news! Congrats, darling!" She gives me a quick embrace and a kiss on the cheek before she turns to her husband again. "Well, if you're done with business for the day, are you ready to take these two gremlins on the slopes?"

Calista waves her phone at her father. "Dad, I've mapped out the slopes I wanna try. Max said he wants to stick with you, but I don't want to do the hard runs. Can I head out on my own? I'll keep my phone zipped and my beeper on."

Marcus smiles at his daughter before pulling her close. "Yes, squidge. That's fine. You go and do your own thing. Only seventeen and already too good to hang out with your old man." He ruffles her hair.

Calista squawks in protest, batting his hand away while Alexandra loops an arm through mine. "That just leaves us. Let's check out the shops and sign up for a few spa packages. I know your future hubby can afford it." She winks at me like we've been friends for ages. "Besides, I can't wait to hear all about your wedding!"

I look at Jack, pleading for his help, and he pulls me out of Alexandra's hold so he can whisper in my ear as he holds me in what appears to be a loving embrace. "Don't worry about cost. Just charge everything and anything. We will talk about this later." He kisses the crown of my head before walking out the door with Marcus and his twins. And all I can do is watch them go.

"Ready?"

I turn back around to see Alexandra waiting for me at the door leading to the other side of the resort, and I swallow down my anxiety. *Why do I always do this to myself?*

"Let's go!" I plaster a smile on my face and follow her through the door.

We walk silently down the hall while I take in my surroundings. Large windows grace either side of the walkway, showcasing the picturesque Colorado landscape. Despite my loathing for all things cold, I have to admit it is breathtaking.

"I've never been fond of snow, but this place is gorgeous," I say, breaking the silence.

Alexandra takes a second to look out the windows with me. "Yeah, I love this place. We vacation here every year around this time. I didn't grow up with the best home life, so I told myself that when I marry and have kids, I'll do whatever it takes to make the best memories. I was a waitress when I met Marcus. He was in town on business and happened to have a meeting in the restaurant where I was working."

She takes a deep breath and continues.

"I wouldn't give him the time of day at first. I figured he was just like all the other businessmen who come in and out of town. You know the type, just looking for a slap and a tickle and nothing serious. While I was no wilting flower, I was determined that my next relationship would be my last."

Her eyes go dreamy as she reminisces about the past.

"He came into that restaurant every night for a month. He refused to sit in any section that wasn't mine, and if I wasn't working, he would leave. The other girls were gossiping about it. They figured I was sleeping with a wealthy man for money. The rumors kept spreading until I finally confronted him."

Alexandra chuckles at the memory.

"I just went off on him. Threw his plate in his lap. Accused him of starting the rumors himself. It turns out he wanted to get to know me, and I'd been refusing to give him my number, so he came in every night because I was stubborn. When he heard about all the insults being slung my way, I'd never seen anyone look so terrifying in my life. He laid his napkin on the table, tipped me a ridiculous amount even compared to his previous tips, and left."

I gasp. "He left! Just like that? After everything you told him?"

Alexandra nods. "I was suspended from work for blowing up at a customer. We were a high-end restaurant, and things like that *just aren't done here* because *we are not a diner or a reality TV show*. Three days later, my manager called, claiming that my suspension had been revoked by the new owner, and asked if I could please come in as they were short-handed. I was confused. We were fully staffed. But then when I got to work, I discovered that the new owner had fired every girl involved with spreading those rumors about me. That's when I realized that Marcus went out and bought the restaurant just to fire the girls who were mean to me."

"That is insane!"

Alexandra and I walk into the gift shop—if it could even be called that, as it closely resembles a mini-mall.

"Oh, yes. It's totally insane, but at that moment, I realized how much he was willing to do just to see me happy. I had never had that in my life. I looked over every interaction and came to the conclusion that he made it known he was interested but was always respectful."

She pauses for a moment before continuing.

"It was everything when I put it all together. All the small things he'd been doing for me. It was everything I told myself I wouldn't settle for *less than*. He'd given me his number weeks prior, but I'd never used it." Her lips quirk. "I never threw it away either. So, I texted him just one word. *Yes*. And he immediately replied with *turn around*. When I did, I saw that he was standing behind me. I threw myself at him, and we haven't looked back since."

"That's amazing. It's like a fairy tale!" I'm in awe. You don't hear stories like theirs every day, and the fact that they are still going just as strong seventeen years later baffles me.

Alexandra walks up to a rack of sweaters, flipping through them before moving onto a wall of boots. "What about your Jack? How did y'all meet?"

I waffle back and forth between responses in my head, deciding to settle on a watered-down version of the truth. "My Uncle Gio. I needed a place to complete my internship hours, and Jack desperately needed someone to handle his desk. He'd run off the last three assistants in a matter of days. I took the job, which allowed me to get my internship hours and whip the office into shape. There was some drama with a girl at first, but things have been smooth sailing ever since. There was so much work at the beginning as he was double and triple booking himself, and projects were terribly behind. Everything is all straightened out now. We are actually ahead of schedule by a month."

"Sometimes all it takes is a woman to come in and clean things up!" Alexandra declares, pulling a pair of knee-high boots off the wall. "These are adorable. I think I'm going to try them on." She scans the shop, looking for an associate.

"When I started, I was worried about proving myself, even though I was insanely overqualified. I still wanted to prove it to myself and my family." I choke over the last word. "I'd heard the rumors and was terrified, but with every meeting, every late night where he ordered me food and made me eat, I saw something different." It shocks me just how much of what I'm saying I actually mean.

"He was different."

I nod, agreeing with Alexandra's conclusion. *He was different.* "Yeah. Are you going to try on the boots? You should. They're super cute!" I say, attempting to steer the conversation in another direction.

"I think I am. You should grab that blue sweater behind you. It would make your eyes pop."

I grab the sweater in question and look at the price tag, almost swallowing my tongue. Five-hundred dollars for a shirt that feels like it was made of clouds and angel wings. "How do you even wash it?" I mutter to myself, looking for the care instructions.

A saleswoman walks up and takes the hanger, crooking a finger while indicating for me to follow her. She looks me up and down before heading toward the back of the store. She stops on the way and picks up some black pants and black boots with heels that, frankly, have me concerned about my ability to walk in them.

When we end up in the lingerie section, I pull up short. She grabs a silver lace garment and then opens a changing room door. She hangs her selections on the little hook and gestures for me to enter. I do as I'm instructed, and she closes the door behind me.

"Well, that was weird." I pull down the silver lace garment and find out it's a silk and lace bodysuit... in my exact size. "How did she do that?" I wonder out loud as I get out of my regular clothes and start putting on the outfit the sales lady chose.

The material is cool, making me break out in goose bumps. I bite my lip, holding back a moan at the feel of the lace against my skin. I've never owned anything so decadent in my life. The rest of the outfit fits as perfectly as the bodysuit, and I'm impressed. Even the boots are comfortable and easy to walk in. I exit the dressing room and stand in front of the tri-fold mirrors, turning side to side to view myself at every angle.

"Girl, that looks amazing on you! You have to buy it! You can wear it to dinner tonight! Jack is going to break his neck when he sees you!" Alexandra gushes, walking up to me with a couple of shopping bags hanging from her arm.

I smooth my hands down the sweater. "Yeah, I think I just might."

"Go change. We'll grab some lunch before we meet the guys." Alexandra resumes her browsing, and I take off my outfit.

Removing the bodysuit feels almost like a sin, and I jump when someone knocks on the door. Then the sales lady walks in, lifts my sweater, snips the tags off the bodysuit, smirks at me, and walks out again.

"That woman is scary," I grumble as I change back into my regular clothes over my new bodysuit.

When I return to the register, the sales lady takes the items to fold and bag. "Name on the account?"

Hearing her voice for the first time has me fumbling over my words. "Maisie Mitchell?"

The woman appears unfazed by the fact my answer comes out more as a question, simply nodding before she begins ringing up the clothes. I watch the total climb and feel myself starting to panic. She hands me the slip to sign, and I gulp at the $2500 price tag but sign it anyway. Worst-case scenario, I can pay Jack back over time.

Alexandra chatters away as we walk back into the dining room where we first met this morning. A waiter seats us, and as we peruse the menu, the conversation is steered toward my fake engagement. "So, what are you planning on doing for your wedding? Have you looked at venues and all that?"

"Well, I want to get married in Australia so my nan can attend." I'm shocked to find the truth in this statement. I never really considered it before I foolishly opened my mouth.

"That makes sense. What about your mom? Is she in Australia too?"

"My mum passed away when I was young. I wish she were able to attend." I feel the tears starting, and I wipe at my eyes, pressing my hands against my cheeks.

"Oh. My darling, I'm so sorry. I had no idea." Alexandra places a comforting hand on my arm.

"It's okay. It happened years ago. Still, it hits differently with the engagement and everything now." I sniffle before forcing myself to laugh. "Okay, enough of me being a sad sack. Let's order!"

Alexandra chuckles as we return our attention to the menus.

Chapter 16

Jack

I watch as the girls walk away arm and arm until Marcus claps a hand on my shoulder. "Don't worry, old bean. She'll be just fine. Your credit card on the other hand? Eh."

I join him in a good-hearted chuckle before we head outside to the equipment shop to rent a set of skis. We strap up, and I follow him to the lifts. The twins grab the one in front of us, and as we're carried up the mountain, I have to whistle at the majestic view.

"Yeah, it's pretty amazing. We come here yearly, and it still takes my breath away."

"I don't think I've ever seen anything so beautiful." Even I can hear the awe in my tone.

Marcus nudges my side. "Except that fiancée of yours. She really is a lovely girl. You look good together."

"Thank you. Maisie is something else. I was a mess before she came into my life." I jokingly recount the early days of her employment, when she straightened out my calendar and had all my project managers terrified to be underprepared for our meetings.

Marcus and I laugh as we dismount. Calista waves at her father before heading off for a less-challenging run while the rest of us make our way toward a more complex one.

We ski for several hours, and I have the best time. It's been ages since I did anything so physically taxing and yet liberating. When we converge at the lift again, Calista is already there at the little cafe, tapping away on her phone.

"Dad… Jenny and Tabitha are here. They want to go to the theater tonight. Can I go with them?"

"What's the featured show?" Marcus ruffles his daughter's hair, peering at her device and wrinkling his nose. "*Twilight*? Really?"

Calista rolls her eyes. "Daaaaaad. Edward's hot. Jenny is Team Jacob, but she's obviously wrong."

"Obviously," Marcus deadpans. "Yeah, you can go. Straight to the room after unless you get permission." He kisses her head, and the girl hops up and is on her way back to the lodge before he can get another word in.

"Dad, I'm going to head back with Calista. A bunch of us are going to hit up the arcade."

Marcus fixes his son with a stern look. "Maxim…."

"I promise, Dad." The kid crosses his heart with his fingers, and Marcus shakes his head.

"Fine. This is your last chance and only warning." Using two fingers, Marcus gestures to his eyes before turning them toward Maxim.

"Message received, Dad. Thank you!" Maxim rushes after his sister, and we grab a seat and a coffee after returning my skis to the rental booth.

"Maxim fell in with a group of boys here at the resort last year. They weren't the usual crowd, and there were some…" Marcus pauses before continuing. "…issues that ended up involving the authorities. Thankfully, it didn't affect our membership to the resort, because we're in excellent standing and have earned our tenure. The other families weren't so lucky. We paid the restitution, and Maxim was made to work off the remaining incidentals, instead of enjoying the rest of his vacation. The lesson seems to have stuck, but we still worry."

"The fact you worry means you're a good parent. Bad parents never worry if they're doing a good job. Trust me, I've seen my fair share of bad ones. I can tell your children love you, and you are definitely a dedicated father." I'm staring at my coffee so intently that I miss the hand clapping on my shoulder.

"Thank you for that. As a parent, you always wonder if you're making the right decisions. What about you and Maisie? Are you planning on having one or two running around soon?" Marcus shakes my shoulder, and I choke on my coffee.

"We haven't discussed it. But not for a few more years, I think." An image of Maisie round with my child flits through my head, and my pulse quickens. I clear my throat. "We were both raised as only children, and we don't want that for our kids, so we would like to have at least two if we're so blessed." This is as good an answer as any and surprisingly accurate.

"We wanted to have more, but when Alexandra got pregnant with the twins, there were complications. We almost lost her. The doctor advised against trying for more. At the time, I was so thankful to have my little family all safe and sound and simply agreed. When the dust settled and Alexandra found out what happened, she was devastated... to put it mildly. It took a while for her to forgive me for that decision and I can't blame her."

Marcus finishes his coffee before stretching out his back.

"There will be days like that in your marriage too. Where you're so mad—no, not mad—*disappointed* in the other person that you just don't think you will be able to see the light of day anymore. And when those days come, and they will, you have to remember why they were your light to begin with."

We sit in silence for several minutes before Marcus stands.

"We better get back to the resort and see what damage the ladies have done on our finances."

We arrive back at the lodge fifteen minutes later. My chest is tight until I see Maisie again. She's sitting at a table chatting with Alexandra. She throws her head back and laughs, and I can feel the band around my chest loosen. I don't know why I was worried in the first place, but she appears to be doing better than okay, if the ease of conversation is any indication.

Alexandra has several bags, but Maisie is sporting one lone bag from the resort shop. I frown a bit before Marcus calls out a greeting, and both women turn to look at us. Maisie's smile is a bit more hesitant, but I still move to the seat next to hers, bending down to brush a kiss against her lips.

"Did you ladies have fun?" I pull my chair close to Maisie and slide my arm around her shoulders.

"We did. I got a few new outfits and a couple of things for later." Alexandra laughs and winks.

Marcus growls in response before pulling his wife close and pinning her with a passionate kiss.

Maisie glances in my direction, uncertainty evident on her face, and I turn to wink at her. "Did you have fun?" I whisper in her ear, and she nods before angling her head into my neck.

"Alexandra is really nice, and I had a good time. I didn't spend too much, so don't worry. I can pay you back." Her voice is breathy and warm against my skin, and I shiver unexpectedly.

"I don't care how much you spent. It's still not enough. And I don't want you to pay me back. After what you're doing for me, please spend my money. Hell, bankrupt me! I can never repay you for this." I brush my lips against her warm, ginger-and-honey skin on the curve of her neck, and her lips part with a gasp. I pull back slightly to look at her. Maisie's pupils are blown wide. Just a tiny ring of blue remains.

A throat clears, and I pull myself back to find Alexandra and Marcus smiling at us.

"My apologies." I grin, and Maisie buries her face in my shoulder.

"No, no. No apologies necessary. Would you like to join us for dinner? You may want to go to your cabin to freshen up, but I would love to discuss the contract more this evening. If you need to, you can borrow our

Outback. That way, you don't have to worry about getting wet and cold." Marcus stands, and I stand as well and shake his hand.

"I'm sure my fiancée appreciates the offer. She's not a fan of the wet and cold." I chuckle when Maisie vehemently agrees with me.

"Oh, no, he's right. I am not a fan. It's beautiful, but I would much rather be warm and dry."

We share another laugh before Marcus tosses me his keys.

"Maisie can drive the Outback and I'll take the snowmobile to the cabin. We'll meet you back here at about eight?" I check my watch and notice it's almost four.

"See you then!"

We make our way to the lobby, and I help Maisie get suited up again. When she resembles a puffed-up bright-pink penguin, I chuckle and lead her outside. The valet takes the key before scanning the QR code and bringing the Outback up to the curb. I help Maisie into the driver's seat and adjust it so she can see.

"Follow me back to the cabin. Don't slam on the brakes. Tap them."

Maisie rolls her eyes. "Just because I don't like snow doesn't mean I don't know how to drive in it. That said, I will make sure that nothing happens to our borrowed vehicle. Promise." She crosses a finger over her chest, and I snort at her sass.

"C'mon, then." I walk over to where we parked the snowmobile, which thankfully cranks up the first time after I unplug the block. And then we carefully caravan our way back to the cabin.

Chapter 17

Maisie

I walk back into the cabin and immediately make tea. My nan always said every problem could be solved with a clear head and tea. My head was anything but clear right now, so the tea needed to step up its game.

The kettle is boiling when Jack makes it into the house from hooking up the vehicles. He's strangely quiet, which only makes my nerves worse. He walks over and rekindles the flame before joining me at the bar. I set the tea in front of him, and he sips. We sit here, for what seems like hours, the crackling of the fire the only sound. Finally, I can't take it anymore and slam my cup on the bar.

"Look, I'm sorry—" I start before Jack interrupts me.

"Thank you." His voice is subdued but steady.

My jaw hits the benchtop. I take a moment to gather myself, but Jack continues before I can say anything.

"I know you only said what you said to help me. Asking you to keep up the charade... I know it's not fair, especially to you. The fact that you are willing to do this for me means more than you will ever know. I keep trying to think of a way to repay you and nothing seems to match what you're doing for me. One thing is certain, though, and that's the fact that I do not deserve you, Maisie Mitchell."

I gape at him. Out of all the things that could have come out of Jack Foster's mouth, that was not what I expected. Which is why I blurt out such a ridiculous response. "I spent $2500 on one outfit."

Jack chuckles. "After what you are doing for me, please spend my money."

"Jack! That's a lot of money. You can't be serious!" I look at him like he has three heads, but his eyes soften, and he cups my jaw.

"I like how my name sounds coming out of your mouth. And, yes, I am serious. I don't want you to worry about money—what you buy, when, or why. I want you to do whatever you want whenever you want. I imagine you and Alexandra will spend a lot of time together on this trip." Jack winks at me before dropping his hand. "Now, we both have to prepare for dinner today, and I don't know about you, but I could use some downtime. That said, we have to go over a few things first."

Jack finishes his cup of tea and places it in the sink. Then he holds out his hand to me. I take it, and he pulls me close.

"We have to make this convincing, so we need to get used to touching each other."

The combination of his voice whispering in my ear and the warmth from his body causes goose bumps. Jack Foster is a potent man, one reason I've always tried to keep my distance.

"Yes, w-w-w-we should do t-t-hat. Y-y-eah." I'm stuttering, and I hate it. I haven't stuttered since I was fourteen. When my crush, Paul Nobleman, asked me to the junior high prom.

When I lean into Jack, his hand on my jaw softly turns my head, and he brushes his mouth over mine. "Oh, Maisie. What am I going to do with you?"

The words glide across my lips like silk, and I sway on my feet. Jack's free hand slides around my waist and pulls me flush against him. I can feel the heat in my cheeks. "Jack?"

He smells like cedar and cherries. It's addicting, and I bury my face in his sweater. I stand here for a minute before trying to step back. No matter how good everything feels, I have to remember this is just a part I'm playing... *and* a mess I got myself into.

"I agree that we need to be more comfortable, but we should reserve that kind of... familiarity for when we're at the resort. When we are here, we should maintain some professionalism."

Jack chuckles low in his throat, and I can't help but shiver. "Oh, but sweet, sweet Maisie, haven't you ever heard the saying *practice makes perfect*? We have to sell our engagement to McIntyre. He's smart, so we have to be convincing."

"Hilarious." I shove at his chest, and he releases me slightly.

Jack buzzes my lips with another kiss before dropping his arms and allowing me to back away slowly. "I'm not joking, Maisie. You may have started this charade, but I'm fully committed to seeing it through."

I watch in a daze as Jack heads upstairs. "What on earth have I done?" I whisper to the empty room.

I place my cup in the sink and head upstairs to prepare for tonight. Sorting through the clothes I brought, I pull out a cream wool dress and pair it with my favorite burgundy wool-lined tights. If I'm going to continue to pretend to be Jack Foster's fiancée, then I'm at least going to be the real me while doing it. I forgo my regular Uggs for the new boots I purchased today. The bodysuit stays on, and at this point, it's so comfortable, like a second skin. I think I may wear it to my grave.

I straighten my hair and apply makeup, then make my way down the stairs again. I find Jack at the bar. He glances up at my approach and does a double-take before walking up to me and taking my hand to twirl me around.

"You look lovely." His lips brush my cheek, and I don't flinch. Instead, I lean into Jack's warmth. "So, it did help."

I pull back, my face scrunched up in confusion. "What?"

"Earlier." Jack walks back to the bar, snapping his briefcase closed. "I purposely pushed my way into your comfort zone so you would get more accustomed to my touch. We don't have any margin for error, and I needed you on board more quickly. It seems to have worked. Are you ready to go?"

My head jerks back like he struck me. "You-you did that on purpose?"

Jack turns around and walks toward the front door. "Of course. Remember, you started this. Don't take that as me not appreciating it, though. It may be the only thing that saves the deal. However, to make it believable, we need to be able to act the part."

Growling, I stalk up to him and poke him in the chest. "Just remember, Jack, turnabout is fair play, and I don't play fair." Then I flick his tie, yank open the door, and head out.

It's going to be a long, long night.

***

Walking into the resort, we meet a very enthusiastic Alexandra and a rather amused Marcus.

"Please forgive my wife. She's excited because the teens are off doing their own thing, and she's made reservations with the theater. They're showing—"

Marcus gets cut off by Alexandra's enthusiastic squeal. "Only my all-time favorite movie ever! *Gone with the Wind*!"

I shoot a pleading look to Jack, and he extracts me from her grasp. "Sounds amazing. It'll keep you ladies occupied while we talk about the boring stuff."

I grumble because business isn't *boring* to me, and Alexandra is a partner in McIntyre Inc. I'm a bit shocked that Jack's pawning me off to watch an ancient movie when I could talk business with them instead. I force myself to unclench my jaw and wrap my hand around Jack's arm, squeezing until my knuckles turn white.

"I don't think I've ever seen that film. It should be fun. Shall we head to our table?" Jack chokes out before unwinding my hands and leading me into the dining room.

We settle in our seats, and I open the special menu. Duck rolls are listed under the appetizer offerings. My stomach growls at the prospect. I love duck. I've only had it a few times, since the dish was usually out of our price range. Still, on my tenth birthday, my mum took me out to celebrate hitting *double digits.* She said it was the first step to becoming a lady and should be celebrated. I smile slightly as I read the rest of the menu.

"What has that smile on your face?" Jack's breath is warm against my ear, and I suppress a shiver.

"Duck rolls."

"I don't understand."

"You asked what made me smile. It was the duck rolls, and I don't expect you to understand." I lean back and return my attention to the menu.

Jack huffs under his breath but then gets pulled into a conversation with Marcus. I look around at the grand windows showcasing the majestic mountains, which are presently bathed in the setting sun. It's all so breathtaking. I never thought that I would be somewhere as unique as this.

Then I return my focus to everyone at the table. Marcus and Jack argue good-naturedly over the nuance of a sentence. Alexandra is on the phone with Calista, who's apparently upset with Maxim. The overall mood is warm and friendly—something I haven't felt in several years.

The waiter's approach incites a flurry of orders, including wine samples and shared appetizers.

I feel an itch between my shoulder blades, as if someone is watching me. I turn toward Jack but don't see anyone paying us any mind beyond the wait staff. I rest my cheek on Jack's shoulder, and he leans in to my touch.

"You okay?" His breath is warm against my cheek, and I can smell the cherries in the wine he's drinking.

"Yeah. I just thought I felt someone watching us."

Jack's head snaps up, his eyes scanning the dining room before landing back on me.

"I don't see anyone. Maybe I'm just being paranoid." I shrug.

"You lovebirds okay?" Alexandra winks, and I grin back.

"Just fine. Are we ready for dessert?" I move the dinner along.

We finish our meal, down our cups of coffee, and then Alexandra is dragging me behind her while I glare daggers at Jack, who's still seated at the table.

He winks at me and shrugs. I vow he will pay for this. I feel eyes on me again and glance around the dining room before the feeling disappears.

By the end of the movie, I'm champing at the bit to hear how the meeting went. Alexandra mentioned this was the movie she and her mum used to watch when she was little, which is why it had such sentimental value. I understand attaching sentiment to things. I do the same thing with vegemite, proper tea, and biscuits.

Marcus and Jack are waiting for us in the lobby when we leave the built-in theater.

"Ah! There they are!" Jack walks up, holds me close to his chest, and kisses me.

I allow myself to get lost in his kiss, which is ridiculous, since we're only putting on a show. A small part of me wonders what it would be like to be fully loved by someone like Jack Foster.

"Did you ladies have fun?" he asks, and I nod before stretching out my back.

My dress and tights are comfortable, but I'm not used to spending over three hours in a plush chair and want to move around to restore my circulation.

"Why don't you two lovebirds head back to your cabin? We can all meet up again tomorrow for breakfast, some spa packages for the ladies, and the sauna for us gents. Then we can discuss the ROI and profit-sharing percentages at greater lengths." Marcus lifts an eyebrow at Jack, who nods in return.

"Sounds like a great idea to me. We'll head out and let you get on with your teen-free evening." Jack grins before taking my hand and heading to the valet stand.

I can sense Marcus and Alexandra watching us, so I lean into Jack, pull his face down, and slide my lips over his. I kiss him slowly, savoring the warmth of his mouth against mine. His hand tightens around my palm, and I feel his heartbeat quicken, matching the fluttering excitement in my chest.

When we break apart, I notice that his eyes are dark and intense while a mischievous smile plays on his lips. "Trying to make them jealous?" he whispers, his breath hot against my ear.

"Maybe," I murmur back, my fingers tracing a path down his chest. "Or maybe I just wanted to kiss you."

He chuckles a low, throaty sound that shivers my spine. "Well, don't stop on my account."

I laugh and pull him closer for another more urgent and profound kiss. The world around us seems to fade away, leaving just the two of us in our little bubble of heat and desire. The valet stand seems a million miles away as we lose ourselves in each other.

A discreet cough breaks the spell, and we reluctantly pull apart, turning to see the valet holding out the keys to the car. Jack takes them with a nod, and we share a secret smile as we walk to the waiting vehicle, our fingers intertwined. Jack starts the engine, and we drive away. I glance back to see Marcus and Alexandra still watching us, their expressions a mix of envy and amusement.

Chapter 18

Jack

I walk into the cabin and take off my suit jacket. Maisie shuts and locks the door before sauntering over to me, sliding her hands up my chest to play with my tie.

"How was the movie?"

She shrugs her shoulders. "Oh, it was just wonderful, Jack. Three hours of epic romance while you were making business deals without me." Her tone drips with sarcasm, her fingers tightening around my tie before she yanks the Windsor knot straight up to my Adam's apple.

"Maisie, come on. It wasn't like that," I choke out, desperately trying to wedge a finger between my neck and the tie.

Despite having to stand on her tiptoes, Maisie doesn't seem bothered by our height difference. "Wasn't it? You left me with Alexandra to watch *Gone with the Wind* while you went off and closed a deal we were supposed to handle together."

I can tell this has gone beyond teasing when her accent bleeds through. She's genuinely upset.

"I thought you enjoyed your time with Alexandra. I didn't think it would bother you this much. Besides, the deal isn't anywhere near closed, and you know it." I finally manage to loosen the tie, and Maisie steps back.

Her glare makes me flinch. "Enjoy? Jack, I was bored out of my mind. And more importantly, I was left out of something crucial. We agreed to work as a team. You can't just push me aside like that. I'm the entire reason we're here. If I hadn't found out that Marcus was going to be vacationing in Aspen, the deal would have been dead where it stood, and you know it! That's the really upsetting part! You drag me to this frozen wasteland, claiming that you can't close the deal without me, and then you leave me out of the discussions while I'm forced to watch a movie with his wife!" Maisie shouts.

"I didn't mean to push you aside." I actually feel bad. When Marcus and I made the plans, we thought the women would be bored and would prefer spending time with each other, not talking shop. I didn't realize it would upset Maisie like it has.

"We've been preparing for weeks. I could have contributed, Jack. But instead, I was sidelined." Maisie's voice drops to a whisper, and I see the tears swimming in her eyes.

"You're right, Maisie. I should've included you. I messed up, and I'm sorry." I pull her close again after removing my tie, just in case. I hold her against me and can hear her sniffling.

"Sorry's not enough, Jack. I need to know you see me as an equal partner in this, not just someone you can shuffle off to the side when it suits you. I know it's my fault we're playing this charade. And I know that, in the long run, I'm no one to you, but I am someone when it comes to this deal. I deserved to be there."

"I do see you. I promise it won't happen again." Her hair is soft as silk under my chin, and I take a deep breath, enjoying her lavender and mint scent.

"It better not. Next time, we will handle things together. No more surprises." Maisie holds up a pinkie.

I return the gesture and chuckle. "Agreed. Together from now on."

She steps back, gazing up into my eyes. Whatever she sees there seems to reassure her. "Good. Now, let's figure out how to proceed with this deal."

Maisie walks into the kitchen, snags a candy cane from the side table, and pulls down the hot chocolate. Shaking my head, I follow along while catching her up on what Marcus and I discussed while she was at the theater.

In true Maisie fashion, she has her steno out and takes copious notes. She wrinkles her nose when she has an idea, causing the light sprinkling of freckles to disappear. When she thinks, she chews on her eraser. And I quickly realize that watching Maisie could become a habit I don't want to give up.

"What do you think?" she mutters to herself and flips through the contract. Then she shakes her head and picks up a highlighter. "Based on the talks you've had today, I believe this paragraph will be troublesome." Maisie turns the contract around, and I find that she's highlighted the sections on profit sharing and intellectual rights.

"Why?" I have a gut feeling I know why Marcus might want to revise the profit-sharing paragraph, but the intellectual rights paragraph gives me pause.

Maisie taps her pen against her steno in a rhythmic pattern while staring into the distance. "Well, Marcus isn't going into this looking at profit. Not initially. He has more money than Croesus as is. He's looking at how and when the profits are divided. His employees benefit from profit sharing at his company, so taking the capital we require away from the company will reduce the amount disbursed to his employees. He'll want to know when this will be recouped. He'll need to get it approved by his board of trustees anyway."

She pauses to take a breath.

"Secondly, in the intellectual rights clause, we have it mentioned as being mutually exclusive, which initially made sense. However, with all the changes you've made, I'm almost positive he's going to want a buy-out option. If the partnership were to dissolve, he'll want a clean break. Like he did with his brother's company five years ago. They had a falling out over how his brother ran things, mainly because he *ran* it into the ground. There were also rumors that he was cheating on his wife with the female employees and then paying them off. Simon had to amass a large chunk of change to buy Marcus out of the rights."

The tapping of Maisie's pen on the steno stops, and I have to shake myself out of the trance the metronome tapping caused. "You got all that from one conversation I summarized and another read-through of the contract?" I'm shocked and can't keep it out of my voice. I always knew that Maisie was brilliant, but this is next level, so imagine my surprise when she shakes her head.

"No, I got that from the conversation you summarized, a reread of the contract, *and* the intel I gathered after researching Marcus when we initially approached him. Seeing that he'd been in business with his brother before ending their partnership abruptly had me looking deeper into the company and why Marcus may have wanted an escape route. I will acknowledge that much of what I found is gossip and conjecture. Still, my mom always said that if you look closely enough, there's a kernel of truth in the gossip, no matter how small. It was just a logical conclusion for me." Maisie shrugs.

Standing, I cup her jaw and pull her up against me. "I'm in awe of you," I whisper before my mouth covers hers and I card my fingers through her hair to cup the back of her head.

Maisie gasps, and I take that chance to deepen our kiss. I never meant for it to go this far, but now that it has, I don't think I can stop. Maisie makes mewling sounds in the back of her throat, and I groan in response. I back her up until her rear hits the cabinet. Picking her up, I deposit her onto the counter and push my way between her legs, causing her dress to ride up even higher.

Her arms wrap around my neck, pressing her body closer to mine, and I feel my throbbing cock notched at her core. I groan at the growing heat between us, and she rubs against me mindlessly, her eyes closed in pleasure. I slide my hands up her ribs, gripping her breast. I cup, feeling her peaked nipple against my palm.

"Tell me to stop." I wrench my mouth away. Panting as I try to form words. "Tell me to stop, and I will." I rest my forehead against hers, my eyes closed and every fiber of my being begging her not to say it. Not to stop this.

"Don't stop." Her voice is breathless.

I growl and band my arms under her ass, scooping her up and heading for the stairs. "Oh, darling. You did it now." I take the steps two at a time, thankful for my workout routine.

I make it to my room in record time, gently tossing her onto the bed. Maisie bounces and laughs until she catches my eyes. I can only assume I look wild. I'm desperate to get my hands on her. I start unbuttoning my shirt, and Maisie tugs at her boots. I wrench the material down my shoulders and throw it behind me as I stalk forward and climb over her. I nip at her chin, nose, and earlobe.

"There is still time, sweet Maisie." I pause before continuing. "You can walk away now. No harm, no foul. Nothing would change between us. However, if you stay, my sweet Maisie, everything will change. Are you sure that's what you want?" I know my grin is feral, but I can't help it. I hold my breath, waiting for her answer.

Chapter 19

Maisie

I can't think. I can't breathe. All I want is for Jack to keep touching me. When he kissed me in the kitchen, shock tore through my every nerve ending. But then that kiss ignited something. And now, if he doesn't finish what he started, I may very well scream.

"Touch me, Jack. I need you!" I wrap an arm around his neck and pull him back to whisper in his ear. "I need you to fuck me, please."

Jack growls. "Oh, sweet, sweet Maisie. You're mine now."

His hands slide up my thighs to the waistband of my leggings, and he rips them down. Hooking my knees, he shoves them up, baring my silk-covered pussy. Jack moans before burying his face between my legs, licking over the silver material of my bodysuit. I may not be a virgin, but in all my twenty-four years, I have never had anything happen to me that was as hot as what Jack is doing right now. He licks and sucks at me. My hips arch as I rub myself against his face.

I hear a noise and can't figure out what it is until I realize the little keens and moans are coming from my own mouth. "Jack, please, I'm so close."

He loops a finger into the suit, pulls the fabric to the side, and slides that finger into my entrance. My muscles clench around him. With a single crook, he rubs over my spongy bundle of nerves, and my upper body jerks off the bed. I come hard and fast, soaking the sheets under me. Jack laps at my pussy with long, broad strokes of his tongue that keep me twitching. Then he shoves my dress up and pulls it over my head.

When he sees the full extent of the bodysuit, he groans a bit more. "Did you buy that today?"

I nod, and Jack catches the zipper on the side, pulling it down with his teeth before removing the garment. I slide my hands along his chest, marveling at the trail of warm skin until I reach his belt. I fumble, trying to open it, and Jack reaches down to assist me. He kicks off the rest of his clothes and stands at the edge of the bed, staring at me. Even though we're both naked, I can feel a blush start to stain my cheeks.

"You're absolutely gorgeous." His tone is reverent, and I bite my lip at the compliment.

"You're not so bad yourself, hot stuff."

Jack barks out a laugh before crawling toward me on the bed. I scramble back until I'm propped on the pillows against the headboard, with Jack kneeling between my legs and staring at me like I'm Rocky Road ice cream, and all he needs is a spoon.

Grabbing my ankles, he jerks me flat onto the bed, covering my body with his. "Are you ready for me, sweetheart?"

Once again, all I can do is nod. I'm so ready for him. I'm borderline desperate, and that desperation bleeds through my garbled, "Please."

Jack hikes my legs up over his hips and notches himself at my entrance, slowly sinking forward. Sliding in an inch at a time, both of us panting and moaning at the sensation.

"Jack," I call out, my voice almost a scream.

"Maisie!" His breathing is ragged, and I see the strain on his face, as if he's trying to hold back and let me adjust. But I don't want that. I want all of him, and I want it now.

"Jack, fuck me like you mean it."

His eyes meet mine, and something he sees there must convince him. Because he grins, sliding back before he rams inside me again.

"Fuccccckkkkk," we both groan in tandem.

"Yes, please, fuck me like that!" I'm not above begging. And, thankfully, Jack is in a giving mood based on his punishing pace as he slams in and out of me.

"God, you feel amazing. Fuck. Princess."

My legs twitch as the head of his cock brushes over that spot again and again. His eyes never leave mine as he licks his thumb before sliding his hand down and finding that bundle of nerves. It takes only a few swipes before I fall apart for a second time.

"Jack!"

He waits for me to fall over the edge first. Then his body tenses as he fills me. Jack collapses on top of me with a groan, his body blanketing mine. He presses a kiss to my temple and rolls over before pulling me to his chest. I snuggle against him, willing my heart rate to slow down. We lie here in a comfortable silence until a shiver racks my body.

Jack pushes up and pulls a blanket over us. "Are you okay?"

His concern is endearing, and I nod. I feel the pleased rumble echo through his chest. My eyes get heavy and I fall asleep with the smell of cherries and cedar in my nose and Jack's hand on my waist.

***

The morning sun wakes me, and I blink in confusion, looking around an unfamiliar room. The first thing I notice is the heavy arm around my waist, and memories of the night slowly return to me. Jack woke me up twice after that first time and each experience was better than the last. I stretch my deliciously sore body, then roll over to face a sleeping Jack. In the morning light, he looks younger and less stressed.

What does Jack Foster dream about? Could he be dreaming about me?

Sliding up onto my knees, I sling a leg over and straddle his lap. The feel of his morning wood against my center makes me throw my head back and moan.

"Now that is how to wake a man up." Jack's voice is rough with sleep. I rub myself against him, teasing him against my entrance before moving away. "Maisie. Don't tease."

I grin down at him, and he reaches up and pinches my nipples. I moan, my head falls back, and I feel my hair brushing my ass and his legs. Two rough hands grab my hips as Jack repositions me and slams upward.

"Jack!" I cry out, jolting against him.

"You thought you would wake me up from dreams of your sweet pussy and then deny me? Oh no, sweet, sweet Maisie, this pussy is mine, and I'll take it whenever I want. Isn't that right, darling?"

The punishing pace addles my brain, and I can only nod in response before rasping out a weak, "Please."

Jack chuckles. "Please *what*, Maisie? Please... *this*?" He licks his thumb before swirling it around my clit, causing my legs to jerk around his hips. "Is that what you want, Maisie? You want to come?"

I nod, and his hand stills.

"Well, naughty girls don't get to come just yet."

I shriek as Jack rolls us over, sliding out of me.

"On your knees, ass up, now." He smacks my ass when I don't move fast enough.

As soon as I'm in position, he slams into me, grabbing a handful of my hair to help pull me back against him. Jack follows me over the edge of pleasure, coming in long spurts, splashing warmth into the center of my body. It's absolutely delicious.

"Maisie. Fuck. Princess. This pussy could drive a man insane." His tone is primal. It's possessive, and I feel another shudder rack through my body. "C'mon." Jack rolls away, and I stare after him, ogling his ass. "Let's see about a shower. We still have to meet Marcus and Alexandra for breakfast."

I follow Jack into his en suite. Once the water temperature is set and the room fills with steam, Jack pulls me into the glass stall, backing me up against the cold tiles. Popping open the top of his bodywash, he drizzles the cool gel over my chest before capping the bottle again. He cups my breasts, massaging the soap into my skin while tugging and pinching on my nipples. It feels like there's a direct line between my chest and my clit, which pulses in time with his movements.

Jack snags a nipple between two fingers. At the same time, his other soapy hand slips down my body before settling between my legs. He then slides two fingers into my sheath, using his thumb to apply pressure to my clit. I can feel his cock hardening against my stomach as he continues his lazy assault on my senses. After every tug on my nipple, he presses harder against my clit, his fingers sliding in and out at a slow pace.

"Jack," I pant. I feel like I may die if he stops, but I may also die if he doesn't speed things up.

"Maisie." His tone is light and teasing but tinged with heat. His pupils are so dilated there's only a tiny ring of color. Jack removes his hand from my nipples and starts to stroke his cock in time with the fingers in my pussy. "You want this cock, Maisie?"

He strokes from root to tip, and I can't take my eyes away. He's so long and thick and delicious that I find myself nodding. Suddenly, Jack takes a step back, and I instantly feel bereft. He rinses off and quickly closes the distance again.

"You want this cock, then get on your knees and show me how much." His voice is velvet over steel, and my knees shake as I sink to the floor, grateful for a solid surface under my body.

I cup his cock in my hands before sliding back and forth. Leaning forward, I dart out my tongue to lick the head, and Jack's rough moan fills the small enclosure. I look up at him and see him staring down at me, his eyes blazing. My lashes flutter closed and I open my mouth to take him deeper.

He stops me. "Eyes on me. I want to see every expression on your face as you drain me dry."

I hold his gaze and slide his thick length as far as I can take it without gagging. Hollowing out my cheeks, I start a slow rhythm that will allow me to take him deeper and deeper until he's sliding down the back of my throat.

Jack leans over me with his hands on the tile, his breath coming out in hard pants above me. "Jesus. Fuck. Princess, yes, just like that. You look so beautiful with a mouthful of my cock. Show me how much you love it. Suck me deeper. Yes, God, fuck!"

It's all the warning I get before I feel hot spurts of cum hitting my tongue and the back of my throat. I swallow quickly, not wanting to waste a drop, as Jack shakes and trembles. Then he grabs under my armpits and yanks me up, and my legs automatically go around his waist before he slams into me. How he's still hard, I don't know, but all thought is chased from my mind as the head of his cock relentlessly punishes my pussy.

"You just had to do that, didn't you? You naughty girl. You just had to make me shoot into that perfect mouth. Swallowing it all like the perfect princess you are."

Jack reaches up and pinches a nipple, tugging it while simultaneously biting my earlobe. "Yes, Princess. Come for me. Come all over this cock."

That's all it takes to send me over the edge. I come immediately and so hard that I can't even move. My limbs feel like lead, and I'm almost certain I'll never be able to walk again.

When I tell Jack as much, he laughs and gently sets me on the built-in bench, washing my hair and body, all before cleaning himself up too. I watch in a haze until he's done and the water stops. Jack wraps a towel around his waist, then grabs one to wrap around me and carries me back into the bedroom.

Chapter 20

Jack

I sit on the side of the bed, holding Maisie in my lap as our heart rates settle. Her breath is soft as it puffs against my neck. I'm unsure how long we sit here before I feel a shiver rock her body.

"Are you ready to get dressed? We need to make our way to the resort." I keep my tone soft and my voice low, in case she needs more recovery time. I don't want her to feel like I'm trying to rush off to business, but we need to make this meeting.

"Yeah. I think I can walk now." Her grin is wry, and I match it with one of my own.

Kissing her softly, I slide her off my lap and onto the bed, and we smile at each other for another few minutes.

"Okay. I need to straighten my hair and get dressed. Give me twenty minutes, and I'll be ready. Promise." Maisie wraps the towel tighter around herself and heads to her room.

I hear the soft click of her door before I get up and make my way into my closet, pulling out a pair of black jeans and a corduroy sweater. I make it downstairs and start brewing a pot of coffee. I'm pouring a cup when I notice Maisie come down the steps in well-worn jeans, a camel turtleneck sweater, and knee-high boots that make her legs look like they go on forever.

"One for the road?" I hold up the carafe, and Maisie nods gratefully.

I doctor up a couple of to-go cups, and we head out to the garage. When we make it to the resort, I'm shocked that Marcus and Alexandra aren't waiting for us in the lobby. I admit we're a bit later than planned, but still on time.

Maisie and I sit in the same dining room as last night, and a waiter brings over the brunch menu. I ask him about the McIntyres, and he says he'll get reception to put a call into their room. He also confirms he hasn't seen them this morning. Which is a relief. I'm glad we didn't miss them.

It takes an additional twenty minutes before a red-faced Alexandra and a smirking Marcus show up at our table.

"Welcome! I'm so glad you could join us. I was starting to worry I'd gotten the times wrong." My tone is smug but teasing.

Marcus slaps me on the shoulder. "Of course not, Jack! We just got distracted this morning and lost track of time."

Alexandra's face now matches her hair. She probably wants nothing more than to sink into the floor and disappear. I chuckle, and Maisie grins as we all place our breakfast orders.

The first half of the morning is focused on friendly conversation. We swap funny anecdotes about our lives and see pictures of the twins throughout their school years. Alexandra regales us with a story about the time the twins started an uprising at their boarding school because administration did away with their favorite breakfast muffins. It ends with a round of applause from the whole table.

I glance to my left and notice that Maisie has slowly started to pull the stationery from her bag. She's flipped her steno pad open. It's clear she's reached her social limit and is ready to talk business.

Marcus notices too and taps his index finger on the table while eyeing us intently. "Well, my friends, I know we had a great discussion yesterday. That said, there are still several key elements of that contract..." He gestures to the document on the table. "...that I'm just not going to be able to get on board with."

"Am I correct in assuming you mean the profit sharing and the intellectual property clauses?" Maisie fires back before I can even open my mouth.

"Well, yes. That's correct." Marcus appears shocked by Maisie's abruptness but she presses on anyway.

"Yes, we understand how those may be troubling sections for you. And we are more than willing to negotiate on anything related to profit sharing as well as implement a buy-out clause that's mutually agreeable to both parties. Making these adjustments will quickly resolve those two minor issues and we could have a new contract prepared and ready for signatures by tomorrow."

Marcus taps the table again, studying Maisie with what I feel is a perfect poker face. "Well, you would be correct, ma'am, except for one small thing. I like to get into business with people I know. And while I've enjoyed *getting to know* you two, I don't know either of you well enough to sign on the dotted line, per se. However, if you can get that contract ready and we can agree to the terms by the end of the week, we'll have a deal—*if* I like what I see." Marcus stretches out his hand to Maisie. "Deal?"

Maisie shakes his palm firmly. "I'm an absolute delight, so deal!"

The table breaks out in chuckles, and the small talk resumes like it never stopped.

After a few minutes, I glance at Maisie again. She appears to be scanning the dining room with a weird look on her face. I don't like it very much.

"Are you okay?" I lean in close and can't help but kiss her exposed neck.

"Yeah." Her voice shakes. "Yeah. I'm fine. Just... it's nothing. Never mind."

I look at her sideways but shrug my shoulders. I'm not going to make her tell me what's going on if she doesn't want to.

"Well, this has been so much fun, but *we've* booked a spa appointment followed by mani-pedis." Alexandra stands and snags Maisie's elbow before dragging her from the table.

"Alex has been waiting all this time to steal Maisie away. She really adores the girl. My wife says your fiancée is sweet as sugar." Marcus's smile is indulgent as he stares after them.

"She's sweet... until she's mad. Fair warning, if you hear her accent come on strong, be wary." I rub at my neck while remembering her snit from last night. I do not want a repeat performance.

"A firecracker, that one, I bet. It's always the small ones that you have to watch. I'm not sure, but heard it has to do with them being closer to hell or something."

I chuckle before pushing up from my chair. "So, what should we get up to while the girls are off getting pretty for us?"

Standing next to me, Marcus slaps my shoulder again. "Well, I'm glad you asked. We have reservations at the sauna this morning. Let's go bare that big, beautiful soul." Marcus throws his head back with a hearty laugh before we follow the girls' route.

By the time we make it to the sauna, I'm sure Marcus has only ever been truly serious in business. It's clear he knows most of the staff, if the back-and-forth banter is anything to go by, and we've even landed ourselves exclusive tickets to a concert happening at the resort. Apparently, Cat Ridgeway is playing, and we have had no less than half a dozen offers to go skiing.

As we settle on the cedar benches, I shake my head. "Do you know everyone here?"

"Well, we've been coming here for twelve years. We started when the twins were about five. We wanted them old enough to be able to enjoy it. Then, over the years, we've become regulars. It's an excellent resort with top-notch staff." Marcus shrugs. "So. Tell me about Jack Foster."

I feel myself blanching despite the steam. I clear my throat. "What do you want to know?"

"I noticed you didn't share funny family stories at brunch earlier. Why is that?"

I sigh. I knew this would happen.

Over the course of the next half hour, I tell Marcus all about the abandoned baby who came to be named Jack Foster. How he grew up to attend one of the most prestigious universities on a scholarship for international students. How he would meet a young Gio Santoro. And how the now famous singer was the only reason that naïve college kid made it through those years at Oxford.

By the time I get to the part where my first business was started in the garage of Gio's house while he was on tour, Marcus is shaking his head in awe. "You really are all they say you are and more."

I frown. "What do you mean?"

"Well, word on the street is that you're a bootstraps boy, that you don't take any shit, but you don't give it either. You're the hardest working person in any company you run, and while no one praises your *sparkling personality*, everyone says that you have the best interests of your employees at heart."

I'm flabbergasted. I don't know what to say. I never realized that people felt that way about me. I was occasionally looked down upon because I'm what most consider *new money*. Still, I didn't realize that the scuttlebutt on the town left me in such a favorable light. "Well, we must not be talking to the same people. I'm well aware of my nickname."

"What nickname is that?"

I have to laugh. "Jack Frost."

Marcus's boisterous chuckle echoes in the sauna as we adjust our towels and head to the locker room to shower. "That's hilarious, my friend. One hundred percent hilarious. Come. Let's grab a drink, maybe a good cigar, and discuss this nickname further."

Chapter 21

Maisie

By the time we leave the spa, I've been brushed, plucked, rubbed, and shined until I'm like a new penny. My hair has never been this soft or straight, and whatever makeup magic they worked on my face is worth every cent the moment I see Jack's face when we join the boys at the bar.

What started as a few mixed drinks and conversation quickly turns into shots and a raunchy version of truth or dare. By round three or four, possibly five, I know I'm not getting out of this night without a hangover while Jack, who volunteered to be our designated driver, is completely sober.

"Why are you always so, so…" My alcohol-addled brain can't think of the words, and I grunt in frustration.

"Smart?" Jack offers.

"Savvy?" Marcus volunteers.

"Oh, I know! Sexy!" Alexandra crows despite the glare on Marcus's face.

"Responsible!" I cry triumphantly.

"Because, Princess, I have precious cargo to return to our cabin." Jack glances at his watch. "Right about now."

Marcus has already started steering Alexandra out of the bar as I turn my pout on Jack. "I don't want to go yet." I sound like a petulant twelve-year-old, but I don't care. I'm finally having fun on this trip.

"I know, Princess, but we need to get home and get you to bed with about a gallon of water and some Tylenol."

"You mean paracetamol."

"Same thing, love. Let's go—upsy-daisy." Jack swings me up in his arms when I stumble on the way to the car, depositing me into the seat before reaching over me to buckle my belt. His arm brushes my nipples when he pulls away, and I can't help the hiss that escapes my mouth. His lips quirk, and then he's jogging around to climb into the driver's side.

Not even giving me a chance to navigate the snow, Jack sweeps me into his arms again when we reach the cabin. I take the opportunity to start kissing all the tanned skin I now have access to with my new height.

"Maisie, just let me get you upstairs. Please."

I renew my efforts to get to more of his warm skin and hear him groaning.

"I swear this is punishment for all the bad shit I've done in my life."

I giggle at his words before nipping his earlobe.

"Princess, you're playing with fire. If you're not careful, you'll get burned."

I can hear his threatening tone, but to my fuzzy brain, it sounds like the best idea ever. I shriek when he drops me on the bed.

"Okay, Princess. You wanted my attention, and you got it." Jack yanks me back to the edge of the bed, flicks my buckle open, and has my pants and boots on the floor before I register a location change.

Flipping me onto my stomach, he lands several sharp smacks on my panty-clad ass. I squeal as his hand slides between my legs to lazily stroke me. With a flick of his wrist, he snaps the string on my panties and shoves them into his pocket.

Then, leaning over until he can rub my nose with his, he whispers. "Tell me to stop. Tell me you don't want this, and I will walk away immediately. Tell me."

"I want this. I want this so badly, please."

The grin that graces his lips is borderline feral. He strips my sweater from my body before he pulls the cups on my bra down with his mouth, latching on to a nipple and scraping it with his teeth. My spine arches and my hands grab at the comforter. I don't know if it's the alcohol, Jack, or a combination of both. Still, it feels like he is everywhere all at once, and it's entirely too much.

Yet I want more.

"Jack, please." I don't know what I'm begging for, but I'll pray to the old gods and the new if he can make this ache disappear.

"All you had to do is ask, Princess." His hot mouth trails down my stomach until he reaches my clit, where he gives it hard, quick lashes with his rough tongue. I don't realize how wet I am until slickness coats the tops of my thighs. I lift my hips, trying to gain more friction. I need more. I need something.

"Please," I beg.

Jack slides two fingers into me, slowly pumping them. I'm babbling. I know I am, but I can't stop myself. Jack slides in a third finger, increasing his speed until it reaches a punishing pace. Without warning, he takes his thumb and twirls firm circles over my clit. I shoot up off the bed, screaming my release. It shakes me to my very core, wringing through my entire body. I gasp, trying to get my breath back as Jack slowly brings me down.

"You okay, Princess?"

I nod, and his grin turns smug.

"You want more?" Jack is standing over what remains of my body, lazily stroking his rock-hard cock. And right now, I want that more than anything. "Then get up there and grab the headboard."

I scramble to obey, and I can feel his warmth behind me when I get into position.

"How do you want it, love? Do you want me to take you nice and slow, or do you want to be my dirty princess, my little toy?"

My pulse thuds at his deliciously sinful words because I want to be his toy. I want him to use me, break me, and put me back together again. "Use me," I manage to get out, and the hands that had been caressing my hips clamp down.

"Oh, love. You have no idea what you are in for." He pulls my hips back until I'm slightly leaning with my ass tilted up. I feel the head of his cock nudging at my entrance before he slams to the hilt in one long thrust. Wrapping one hand in my hair, he uses the other one to punish my nipples with tight pinches and pulls.

I buck back against him, moaning and panting. "Please."

"That's it. Beg for me. Show me how much you want this." Jack continues to thrust hard and fast into me, and the pace rocks the bed.

I have a vague thought of being glad that we're the only ones in the house before his hand leaves my breasts and moves down to the slickness between my legs, gathering some before swirling small circles over my back hole.

My head drops forward as much as possible with his hand still gripping my hair. "Fuck. Jack. Please."

"You want me here? Do you want me to fuck this pretty little asshole? My, what a dirty little toy I have." Jack has worked up to his second knuckle while his cock still punishes my pussy. "I wonder what would happen if I just..."

He releases my hair to pinch my clit, and I scream as I fall apart, my body locking as waves of pleasure decimate my ability to even see.

"Oh. Fuck. Shit," Jack grunts as he comes with me. He slams me down on him with a hand around my throat. "I didn't want to come in your pretty pussy, but you pulled it right out of me, didn't you, love? I was going to come in this delicious ass that has been torturing me for months, but you had other plans." His breath is hot against my cheek as we pant through the aftershocks.

Collapsing sideways, Jack tugs a blanket over us again, and I'm asleep before he even pulls out.

***

The following two days are spent with Marcus and Alexandra. They even manage to get me on a slope—albeit the training slope—a time or two. I spend my nights in Jack's bed, where we continue to explore all the different ways we can make each other fall apart.

It's the day before Christmas Eve when we head to the resort. I'm in the lobby sorting some files and waiting for Jack to let me know if our table is ready, when I feel a rough hand on my elbow yanking me to the coat check.

A chill runs down my spine as I stare up into the eyes of the man I have no desire to see again. Especially now. "F-f-father. What are you doing here?" I look around for Jack but don't see him.

"What am I doing here? I belong here, unlike you. Do you think your new friends would like you half as much if they knew you were just a penniless college student who had to blackmail her own father to survive?" When my face goes pale, he grins. "I thought not. Are you fucking him to get back at me?"

"Am I fucking *who* to get back at you? What are you talking about?" I yank my elbow out of his bruising grip.

"Jack. Are you fucking him to get back at me?"

"Why would I fuck him to get back at you?"

My father's cold eyes turn colder. "Are you fucking him for money, then? Is that what this is? Don't think I haven't noticed all the trips to the resort shops and spa treatments. You're just like your mother, latching on to the first wealthy man you can dig your claws into and then trying to baby trap them."

"That's not true! Mum would never have done that!" My voice shakes as I continue to search for Jack in the crowds.

Jack will save me. So where is he?

"Of course she would! I was sixteen! I had my whole life ahead of me! She went and got pregnant and then refused to get rid of it." His sneer makes my blood run cold. "My family had to pay her off to make her go away, and then she just had to go and get herself killed, and I got saddled with you anyway!"

The venom in his voice has me stepping back.

"I don't know why you're here, but you're not going to get anything from me, so I suggest you leave. I may have no love lost for Jack, but he deserves better than the bastard offspring of a teenage whore." My father spits the words at me before turning and stalking off.

My hands are trembling and I can feel the tears pooling in my eyes. I want Jack. If I can find Jack, everything will be okay. I just know it.

"Is that what you were doing?"

I hear his voice behind me, and I spin around, grateful until the look on his face draws me up short. His face is cold, colder than the first day I met him. "Jack, I'm so glad you're here. I just—"

Jack cuts me off. "I know what you just said. You just met with your father. Are you trying to cut him in on this deal to steal it? I'm aware Antony approached McIntyre about a deal, and that it has yet to go anywhere. Did you take the job at my company just so you could spy and report back to him?"

"Jack! No! Why would you think I would even do that?" I reach for him, but he steps back, his hands shoving into his pockets.

"For someone who supposedly hasn't seen her father in years, you were both in this corner looking pretty cozy."

"No, you don't understand—"

Jack cuts me off again, and I can't help the tears that spill down my cheeks. "No. I think I understand perfectly. I don't think *you* understand that I refuse to be used like this. I think it's best if you leave. I don't care what it costs, and I don't care where you go, but I don't want to set eyes on you after today." Jack turns and walks away, and I stand here crying, unsure what to do next.

"Ma'am. Are you okay?" An employee walks up and lays a gentle hand on my arm.

"Oh. I'm... I'm not sure. I need to book a flight. Yes. That's it. I need to book a flight. Do you have a business center? I don't seem to have my laptop with me."

The lady offers me a sympathetic smile before showing me to the business center, where I book the next flight to Sydney. She then helps me arrange a ride to the airport. I glance around one last time, searching for Jack, but I don't see him. I chew my lip while I consider looking for him again, until the expression on his face swims in my mind, and I turn and walk away.

If he can believe something like that about me, he doesn't know me. And apparently I don't know him either.

Chapter 22

Jack

I confirm our table and walk back to the lobby. I see Maisie huddling in the corner with someone. I get halfway across the room when I realize that someone is Antony.

When did he get here?

I stride up to tell him to get lost when I notice how close they are, how they're whispering, and my stomach drops. It's Monica all over again. I didn't learn my lesson the first time.

I knew when I went after McIntyre that Antony had already tried to score a deal with them. But unlike Antony, I know about business trends. While his business failed, mine thrived.

Was Maisie a plant? Gio would never have done something like that to me, but he still has a blind spot for my former friend. Antony could have had Maisie approach Gio about a job, knowing he would send her my way...

Was the poor, pitiful college student routine just an act? Now that I think about it, Antony didn't protest too much when I forced him to send her funds.

The doubts swirling in my mind make my stomach turn. How could I have been so stupid? So short-sighted? I never should have gotten mixed up with anything to do with Antony—especially his daughter.

I head straight to the bar and order three fingers, neat. I sip the burning liquid and stare out over the mountains, while replaying the past week in my head, trying to see where I could have been mistaken and how I could have missed the signs.

"It's a bit early to hit the hard stuff, right?" Marcus walks up, and I do my best to try to grin. Based on the look on his face, I've failed.

"No. It's the right time to be honest. Look, I'm sorry but I think I'll have to reschedule today. Something's come up, and I cannot give this deal the attention it *and you* deserve."

Marcus gives me a skeptical look. "Where is Maisie, Jack?"

I swallow another swig of whiskey before clenching my jaw.

"Jack. I'm going to ask you again. Where is Maisie?"

I shove a hand through my hair and sigh. "It's nothing. Don't worry about it."

"Oh, that's it. Come on, you stubborn ass." Marcus drags me over to a corner table. "Spill."

His tone leaves no room for refusal, and I'm just buzzed enough to obey. So I start with Gio, Antony, and me. Then, move on to Monica and even add in the details of Maisie's parentage.

Marcus is silent for a few minutes until I look up and see the pity in his gaze. "Jack, if you believe half the shit you just said, then there's no hope for you. Anyone with eyes can see that girl is head over heels for you. Now, I'm going to tell you what I saw. I was on my way to the restaurant to get my lovely wife a coffee when I spotted Maisie in the lobby. I was about to approach her when a man walked up and yanked her into the corner by the coat check."

As Marcus recounts the story, complete with the vile threats Antony flung at Maisie, I have to fight to keep myself from throwing up.

"Jack, she was crying when he left. I was coming to find you when I saw you'd already found her. I know now that you have apparently screwed the pooch in a big way." He sighs. "I'm not saying it's all your fault. Extenuating circumstances colored your view of what happened, but I must ask you again, Jack. Where is Maisie?"

"I don't know." It's all I can whisper. "I told her to leave, that I didn't care what it cost, and that I never wanted to see her again."

"Jack, you have to find her. Listen. There's a blizzard coming. You won't be able to do anything until tomorrow. They will have grounded the flights. Let's pack up here and you can stay at the resort." Marcus shakes me by the shoulders. "But first you have to find Maisie."

I can feel the blood drain from my face. A blizzard's coming, and I told her to leave. *What if she tries to drive?*

I lurch out of the chair and run to the valet. Then I drive as fast as the weather permits, not even bothering to kill the engine.

I burst into the cabin, calling her name. Silence greets me. I take the stairs two at a time, flinging open the door to her room. Everything she owns is still here, tucked away in the drawers. I can still smell her perfume lingering in the air from this morning. I pull my phone out of my pocket and dial her number, praying as the call connects. I hear a ringing in the room and look over to see her cell resting on the bedside table.

"Fuck. Fuck." I run my hands through my hair. "Where are you, Princess?"

I hear a noise and hurry down the stairs, stopping abruptly when I see Marcus standing at the bottom. "Is she here?" he demands.

"No. Everything she owns is, though. Even her phone." I run my fingers through my hair again, cursing myself a fool for ever comparing Maisie and Monica. If I find her, I swear I will spend the rest of my life apologizing.

"Shit. Okay, here's what we are going to do. We're going to find Antony at the resort and kick his ass."

"We can't do that, Marcus, and you know it. No matter how much he deserves it. You heard the venom he threw at her. Then I compounded it. And now she's running. I can't blame her. If we're being honest, I wasn't very nice. The whole situation just reminded me of Monica, and when I think about that woman, I lose it."

"I get it. We all have triggers, but right now, we have more important things to worry about, like saving your marriage and fixing this before you lose her forever. Maisie not having her phone makes it trickier. Does she have any friends? Anyone she may have told where she was going?"

"No. She—" I stop. "Stella."

"Stella?"

"We have to go to New York. Now." I turn to the front door, but Marcus catches my arm.

"Hate to tell you, but you're not going anywhere tonight with this blizzard coming on. They're going to be grounding all the flights soon. Let's pack you up, and you can head out first thing tomorrow when the airports open again."

Marcus's tone is coaxing, and while I know he's correct and that the logical thing to do is to wait until the weather clears and I can safely fly back to my office, I want to find Maisie now. I don't want to wait until tomorrow to get down on my knees and beg her for forgiveness. I pick up the nearest ceramic Santa and throw it into the wall with as much force as I can muster, and I have to admit I feel marginally better.

"Fine. Let's do it your way. I'll start packing." I head straight to Maisie's room and fold her belongings into her suitcase. I see her older clothes mixed in with her newer pieces, and I can't help but wince when I remember what that asshole of a father said to her.

Sighing, I continue to pack with care, the same care I should have shown Maisie. One thing's for sure, it's never too late to teach an old dog new tricks.

Jack Foster 2.0 is online, and he's ready to prove just how much he's changed.

Chapter 23

Maisie

When you're on the other side of the country, flight times get exponentially longer. I was lucky that I made it onto the plane before the blizzard hit. My flight was one of the last allowed to take off before everyone else was grounded.

I sigh and thank my lucky stars for always carrying my purse no matter what. I didn't have my mobile, so I had to buy a cheap prepaid at the airport gift shop. But besides that, I have basically everything I *need*.

Now, I'm settling back into my seat. Eighteen hours, and I'll be home. I can't help but think about the look on Jack's face when he walked up after my father—no, *Antony* left. I refuse even to pretend that man was any kind of father to me.

I order a gin and tonic from the stewardess and drink it down in two gulps. I'm heartbroken at how Jack tossed me aside; however, deep down, I also wasn't surprised. I don't know what it is about me, but men have been tossing me aside my entire life. Whatever the reason, I'm officially done. D-O-N-E. From now on, I'll focus on myself and Nan.

I pull the thin airline blanket higher and frown at the scratchy texture, missing the soft microfiber from the cabin. Then I do my best to get comfortable. It's going to be a long flight.

***

Port Stephens, Australia, is a two-hour drive from Sydney and is known for its twenty-six beaches. A sense of peace settles in my soul when I step off the plane. I'm home. I'll heal. There's nothing that can't be fixed with a beach, a wave, and a good stiff drink—at least, that's what Nan has always claimed.

I grab a taxi to the townhouse that Nan transferred into my name when she went into care. I can't feel anything and am freezing despite the heat. I may never get warm again. I don't have any luggage, so I trudge up to the lift, hitting the button for the fourteenth floor. The doors close, and I spend a few minutes staring at my feet.

I punch in the code for the lockbox at the door, grab the key, and head into the townhouse. The air is stale, and I can tell by the thin layer of dust coating multiple surfaces it's been a few weeks since the cleaning company has been by. It doesn't matter to me, so I trudge back to my room, opening the sliding glass door to the balcony. Immediately, the scent of sand and sea fills the space, and a breeze from the ocean clears out the remaining stale air.

I stand at the door for a moment, just watching the waves. For the last three years, all I could think about was getting back here, getting a job that would allow me to support myself and Nan and get her out of that care home. That goal has been EVERYTHING. Every hour I worked, every meal I skipped, was to get to this point.

Now that I'm here, I'm numb.

Antony's words bounce around in my head. The accusations about Mum... I always suspected he knew about me from the beginning, but now I know the truth. He really is a waste of oxygen. For all the vile things he was spewing about my mother, she never said an unkind word about him. She wanted nothing more than for me to have a relationship with my father but knew better than to reach out.

Now I know why. She took the money and ran as far as she could to give me the life that I deserved. She wanted better for me, and then I had to go and fall in love with a man who's the mirror image of my sperm donor.

A Rich. Cold. Conceited. Asshole.

I turn around, walk to the bed, and fall face-first on the mattress. I'm so tired. I just can't anymore. I grab the throw from the end of the bed and catch a faint whiff of Nan's favorite washing powder. The scent breaks me, and once the tears start to fall, they don't stop. I sob for what may be hours before I finally fall asleep with the smell of the ocean and the warm December breeze in my room.

***

I'm unsure how long I've slept, but the sun is below the horizon by the time I wake up, and I have the worst case of cottonmouth. Sitting up, I clutch my throbbing head. I'm dehydrated and jet-lagged.

I stumble into the kitchen and grab a glass, filling it with water from the sink. I gulp three cups full before I finally start to feel semi-human again. I look around the dark townhouse, take a deep breath, and return to the bedroom with a fourth glass of water. I place it on the side table, crawl into bed, and prop myself against the headboard.

I pull out the cheap prepaid mobile from my handbag and open at least twenty text messages from Stella. Not wanting to deal with all of it, I text her to say that I'm safe and that I would message her later. Then I check the time. She's probably asleep anyway. Good. The last thing I feel like right now is talking Stella down from doing something she might eventually regret. Prison orange is not her color. I toss the phone at the foot of the bed and wrap myself back up in the throw blanket.

I have so much to do. The least of which is arranging for all my items to be packed up and shipped from my apartment. I sling my legs out of the bed and head over to the dresser. My old panda pajamas stare back at me from the top drawer. I smile. Nan got these for my eighteenth birthday. It's a running joke between us that I was born on the wrong continent, as we have "the wrong bears" because I love pandas. I don't care how cute the tourists think koalas are. Truth is, they're nothing but Chlamydia-carrying demons.

Stepping into the en suite, I splash water on my face before finally looking at myself in the mirror. My hair is messy, I have bags under my eyes, and my skin is pale. I change into my panda pajamas and throw my grungy clothes in the general direction of the hamper. I can't deal with anything else today. Tomorrow Maisie can have that chore as well. Then I flip off the light and head back to bed.

Tomorrow will be better. It has to be, right?

Chapter 24

Jack

I call the director of human resources to get Maisie's file emailed to me. She has a home address in Brownsville and lists Gio as her emergency contact. Then I wait at the airport and take the first available seat back to New York. As soon as I land at JFK, I grab a town car and head straight to her apartment.

As the driver turns into her neighborhood, I suck in a stuttered breath. It's not the worst area in the city, but it could be better. Maisie has been living here this whole time, and I never knew. Well, this is the first thing that's going to change. Maisie will never live somewhere where she's anything less than absolutely safe, and she will not live somewhere where homeless people piss on the stoops at night.

I find her name on the intercom and lay on the buzzer. Nothing happens. I continue to press the buzzer incessantly but can't tell if it's working. Taking a chance, I push on the door, and it gives without much resistance.

I check my phone for her apartment number and head up the stairs, trying desperately to ignore the faint smell of urine that permeates the hallway. When I make it to her door, I pound my fist against it, loud and long.

"Maisie! Are you there? Maisie, please open the door! Maisie!" I press my palm to the dingy wood, leaning my head against my hand as I plead with her to open up.

"Are you looking for the sweet little piece that lives there?"

I turn toward the voice coming from behind me and find the occupant from across the hall eyeing me from his threshold. Wearing a stained and dirty wife beater and tartan pajama pants that have seen better days while the stench drifting off him is enough to make me vomit into my mouth.

"She's a right sexy piece of work, prancing around in those tight skirts and fuck-me heels, but I haven't seen her for a couple of weeks now. I think she may still be out of town."

"Fuck." I pull out my cell phone and shoot off a text.

"You fucking her?" The waste of oxygen next door looks me up and down.

"Excuse me?"

"I've been working on her for months. I'm so close to getting into that tight little snatch. I don't need some fancy fucker like you traipsing in here and messing things up for—*oomph*." Neckbeard doesn't have time to finish his sentence before my fist breaks his nose. He squeals like a pig. "What-did-ya-do-that-for?"

"If you even think about breathing in Maisie's direction, your nose will be the least of your worries. Do you hear me? I could buy and sell you before lunch and not even break a sweat. Try. Me."

Neckbeard slams the door shut, and I return my attention to Maisie's vacant apartment. I have to search for the superintendent. I can get more information off her rental application. Yeah, he's technically not supposed to give it to me, but if he doesn't, I'll buy the building.

I have her address in Australia by the time I leave the super's office. I also paid off her lease and had my house manager set up a company to pack her things. Now, armed with an apartment key and an address, I head home to pack. I have a flight to catch.

***

I'm standing in the middle of JFK, glaring at the attendant behind the desk. "What exactly do you mean *there are no more flights until after Christmas?*"

The customer service rep's Adam's apple bobs as he swallows down his nerves. "I'm so very sorry, but due to so many last-minute flights, there are simply not enough seats." He swallows again as I lean over the counter and continue to glare at him.

"I have to get to Australia immediately. What do you suggest I do if, as you state, there are no more flights until after Christmas?"

"You could charter a private jet?" the representative stammers.

I slam my hand down on the counter, and more than a few people jump. "You're a genius!"

I whip out my phone and call the one person I know who can get me to Australia before Christmas.

"Gio, it's Jack... Yes, yes, hello. Listen. I need to borrow your plane... Yes... No... I need to get to Australia." Sighing, I lift my eyes to the heavens, asking for intervention. When nothing happens, I go back to the call. "I fucked up... Yes. I know... It was Antony... No, that's on me... I told you. I fucked up... Why should you lend me your plane? Because she's mine, Gio. I love her."

I'm surprised to find that I mean those words. *I love her.* I'm trying to figure out how or when it happened. But the particulars don't matter. I can't imagine waking up and not having her cook in the kitchen, sing Christmas carols, and read a book with a candy cane in her mouth.

"She's everything, Gio. I may not have made the best decisions lately, but she is the best thing to ever happen to me. I will find her again with or without your help, but it'll be a hell of a lot quicker if you just give me a hand."

Something must convince him because he finally relents.

"Gio. I could kiss you, but I don't know where that mouth has been, so I'll have to pass... When are we leaving?" I walk toward the lounge, where he directs me to go, and he promises to call me back after he gets in touch with his pilot. So I settle into a chair and wait.

***

Five hours later, I settle into the plush seat while a smiling pilot does his preflight checks, and an air hostess offers me a drink. "Scotch, if you have it. Neat. One finger."

"Of course, Mr. Foster. Right away."

As she walks towards the back of the plane, I skim my notifications. Gio's texted me a few times, and Marcus has been blowing up my phone for an update. When it beeps, I see an email pop up.

I hired a private investigator to look into Maisie a few weeks ago. Everything she told me combined with what I knew about Antony and his family didn't add up. So, then I had my guy start looking into Antony. I honestly forgot about it.

I click on the email and scan the report on Antony. Which tells me the man's cheated on his wife with several women—a few of them *hookers*. He spends most of his nights and money at high-end strip clubs. He has a kept mistress in an apartment on the more fashionable side of town.

The PI ends with all the information he's found about the state of Antony's business affairs. Everything my former friend owns is in the toilet and has been for a while. I've heard rumors that his last big investments flopped but took them to be just that. Rumors.

The stewardess lays a hand on my shoulder and I look up. "Mr. Foster? We're about to take off now."

I nod, ensuring my seat belt is buckled as we taxi down the runway. I've spent so many years trying to protect my heart from ever being hurt again, but that all changes now.

If anyone on this planet is worth thawing for, it's Maisie Mitchell.

Chapter 25

Maisie

The morning sun shines relentlessly through the balcony doors when I wake up. Wincing, I sit up and drag a hand through my hair. My stomach growls, and I sigh.

I'll have to order in. But I need to shower first.

Once I'm thoroughly rinsed off, I pad back into the living room while browsing Door Dash to see what's available. Many places are closed, and that's when it clicks. It's Christmas Eve. I've always loved Christmas, but this may be the first year that I don't have it in me to celebrate.

I settle on Maccas before switching over to do a grocery order. I'll need candy canes, vegemite, and toast to do this right.

***

After putting away the groceries and devouring a whole Hawaiian pizza later that afternoon, I move toward the living room to settle in when my door buzzes. And I foolishly look around like someone will materialize before quickly pressing the intercom. "Hello?"

"Maisie! Oh, thank God I found you."

I gasp as my finger flies off the button. It's Jack. *How did he find me? Why is he here?*

I push the button again. "What are you doing here, Jack?"

"What do you mean? I'm here for you!"

"Why, Jack? You made your opinion quite clear in Colorado. There was no reason to follow me across the globe just to twist the knife. Go away."

"Maisie. No. Please. Let me explain, baby, please. Let me in."

"No, Jack. I'm done. We're done. The charade is over. Go away." My hand shakes when I release the button, and I sink to the floor, tears streaming down my face again as Jack's voice comes over the intercom one more time.

"I'll go, but I'm not leaving, Princess. I promise I'll prove to you just how wrong you are."

I bite my knuckles to keep myself from caving. Even now, when my heart is shattered, I want Jack near me. I stay put, waiting for him to say something else, but I don't hear his voice again.

Did he leave? I mean, that's what I wanted, right?

"Right." I get up and make myself a cup of tea before settling back on the sofa and clicking on Netflix.

Crazy Rich Asians was recently added, and it feels appropriate. An average person getting swept up in a romance with a handsome, wealthy man, only to find out that things aren't what they seem. At least the movie will end with a happily ever after.

"Indeed."

I've just reached the part of the movie where Nick's mum informs Rachel that she would never be enough for the family when the intercom buzzes again. I slam the pillow down and stalk over.

"I said go away, Jack." I release the button while muttering under my breath.

"Uh, ma'am, my name's Oliver, and I have a delivery here for Maisie Mitchell?"

"I'm so sorry! I didn't order anything for delivery?" I'm mortified but... curious.

"This order was placed by Jack Foster. He paid us triple the going rate to ensure it was delivered and set up today. He even tipped. Can we come up?"

I buzz the guy in, then move to the door, swing it open, and wait. *What in the world has Jack done now?* I know Oliver wants to keep his tip. It's rare in this part of the world.

It takes several minutes before a gentleman with a clipboard lands on my doorstep. "Miss Mitchell?"

"Yes. Oliver?"

"Yes, ma'am. Where would you like it?" He shakes my hand before stepping into the house.

"Where would I like what, exactly?" I follow behind him.

"I think that corner would be best. Bring her in, boys." He points to the corner by the glass wall in the living room.

"Bring who in?" I stutter out before I see two more people bringing in what has to be a six-foot tall live Christmas tree.

I recognize the tag—it's from Santa Trees Christmas Tree Farm. They're the most popular tree farm in the area. The two men with the tree are quickly followed by at least five women pushing a trolley of boxes. I can feel the tears welling up on my lashes when the women open everything up and pull out decorations.

Jack brought Christmas to me.

One of the ladies hands me the box of candy canes, and I'm taken back to the first time I mentioned decorating the office. I'd been lamenting over the lack of candy canes, and Jack tossed me a peppermint. Which led me into a fifteen-minute rant about how peppermint candies are not the same as candy canes and are, in fact, inferior.

I unwrap a candy cane and stick it in my mouth, savoring the sweet peppermint flavor as my house is slowly transformed into a winter won-derland. The scent of pine from the garland fills the air, and the twink-ling lights cast a warm, festive glow while the tiny, extremely expensive

Christmas village is a sight to behold. It's everything I've ever wanted for Christmas at home.

Poinsettias sit in various places, their vibrant red petals adding to the holiday cheer, and the star at the top of the tree twinkles merrily. Exhausted and exhilarated, I collapse onto the couch and stare around my freshly decorated townhome. Until the buzzer sounds yet again, and I jump, startled by the sudden noise in the otherwise quiet room.

"Hello?" I'm so overwhelmed that I don't even want to know who it is.

"Miss Mitchell?" I don't recognize the woman's voice on the other side of the intercom. "My name is Angelique, and I have an order here for you?"

I buzz her up. And when she knocks on the door, I open it to see another full trolley behind her. This one includes various dishes: ham, seafood, mashed potatoes, and cornbread. I also spot pudding, a cake, and multiple red and white wine bottles when Jack only drinks Scotch. The contrast between these offerings and Jack's preferences piques my curiosity. Though I'm well aware this is his attempt to win me over.

That said, I have no idea how he knew what to get. We never, ever talked about Christmas past his disdain and my love of it. No one in the States knew any of this except...

"Stella." I dash back into the bedroom and snatch my phone off the charger. I have one text alert. Opening it, I see a single message.

Stella: Trust me.

Angelique sets up a Christmas feast on the table, smiling the entire time. "That is some man you have there! He called and offered me quadruple my rate if I could have something done in time. He even offered a tip if I delivered and set it up for you. He was adamant that you do not lift a finger. He had this serving set delivered as well. Isn't it just gorgeous?" She holds up a dinner plate with delicate silver snowflakes around the outer edges.

"It really is." I'm choking up and trying really hard not to cry.

I'm standing in my living room when there's another knock on the door. I walk over and open it, and there he is, on my doorstep in a charcoal gray suit that makes his eyes pop. He looks so incredibly unsure that the tears I have been holding streak down my cheeks.

"I'm sorry to just come up, but I caught someone leaving and slipped through. I didn't think you'd let me in if I buzzed again, and I had to see you. I had to make sure that everything was set up just the way you wanted it. I know you'll probably never forgive me, but I had to do something."

His speech is stopped short as I missile into his chest.

"Don't cry, Princess. Please don't cry. I can't stand it. I'll spend the rest of my life making this up to you. Please. Give me a chance?"

I cry harder, hiccupping, not able to do anything but nod. Jack exhales, his head resting on top of mine for a minute before he picks me up and sits on my couch, depositing me on his lap. He presses my face into his chest, strokes his hand through my hair, and just holds me while I cry.

It could have been minutes. It could have been hours, but when the tears finally stop, I can't breathe through my nose, and his jacket is soaked straight through to his shirt.

"Jack, I—"

He cuts me off with a smile. "No. I'm privileged to be here for you in any way you need. It's an honor to be the man you feel safe with. I lost sight of that. I'm sorry. However, I have one more gift in my never-ending effort to make it up to you."

He stands, lifting me in his arms again, and heads to the en suite to gently clean my face. I sit on the vanity top and let him, enjoying being with him again.

"Are you ready for your surprise?"

I nod while biting my lip. Jack sends off a text on his phone before grabbing my hand and guiding me back to the main room. When someone knocks on the door, he opens it, and I see Uncle Gio and my nan standing on the other side.

"Nan!" I dash forward, only to be enveloped by her familiar scent.

"Oh, my sweet lamb. You've been through it, haven't you, love? Jack set it right, then?"

Tears swim in my eyes again as I nod at her.

She kisses my cheek gently. "Good."

"*Cara mia*! Maisie!" Gio wraps his arms around me from behind, and I laugh as he lifts me off the ground.

"Uncle Gio! Stop! I can't! Please!" I'm laughing as he jostles me over to the living room.

When I'm finally standing again, I turn and spot one more surprise. Stella is positioned in the doorway, watching us all with a strange look in her eyes. Then she takes a tentative step forward.

"Stella!" I wrap her in the biggest hug I can manage. "Thank you," I whisper in a voice low enough only for her ears, and she hugs me back.

"You can thank me by introducing me to your hot uncle."

I chuckle, pull back, and do precisely that. The conversation is loud, as it always is with Uncle Gio. Although everyone at the table knows some version of what happened, none of us brings it up again. It's in the past.

We eat while Nan shares funny stories from growing up, including the time I was determined to bring home a quokka to make Mum smile. We had been on vacation on Rottnest Island. Turns out that's a felony, and while the authorities thought it was hilarious, as an eight-year-old, I was scared silly. I spent the entire ride home in tears, fearing I wasn't going to be allowed out of the country because I thought I was a criminal.

Everyone laughs, but Stella immediately has to look up what a quokka is and then demands to know where to find one. We all laugh again, and the festivities continue well into the night before Nan calls it quits.

Uncle Gio hugs and kisses me, escorting Nan back to the retirement community. Stella joins them, since her hotel is on the way. And before I know it, it's Jack, me, and the now-quiet townhome.

Jack walks up, sliding his arms around my waist before tucking my hair behind my ear. "You hurt me," I tell him.

He closes his eyes and sighs. "Yes."

"You can't do that again."

"Never. I will do whatever I can to make it up to you. I know I said it before, but I'm serious when I tell you I'll happily spend the rest of my life making up for my truly heinous behavior in Colorado."

I run my finger under his collar. "Well, I have one idea of how you can make it up to me."

At his confused look, I slide my hand into his and pull him back toward my room. When he realizes where we're going, a salacious grin spreads across his face.

"Oh, Princess. Gladly." Jack sweeps me into his arms, kicks the door closed, and spends the next few hours showing me exactly what he means.

<hr>

Chapter 26

Jack

I wake up to the smell of the sea and a face full of wavy blonde hair. I push it aside and realize that Maisie has migrated over to lay on top of me at some point in the night. I wrap my arms around her soft curves, loving the feel of her against me. Then I inhale her scent and can't stop the smile spreading across my lips.

I almost lost her.

When I got to her place and she wouldn't let me up, I thought I would lose my mind. I had to persuade her to at least talk to me. Then I remembered how she'd left with nothing. It was almost Christmas, and I knew immediately the only way to get her to even think about forgiving me was for me to finally get over myself and my insecurities and give to her like she's been consistently giving to me since the day we met.

Maisie stirs and my smile grows wider. "Good morning, Princess."

Maisie grins sleepily at me, and I kiss her again. Just a light brush of lips. "Would you like a coffee?"

At her sleepy nod, I stand, grab my slacks from the floor, and pad barefoot into the kitchen to fix her a cup exactly the way she likes it. *Blonde and sweet, just like her,* she joked when I heard her coffee order for the first time.

I take the steaming mug back with me to the bedroom a few minutes later and find Maisie upright with a blanket wrapped around her, but her face is serious. "Jack, we have to talk about what happened. You claim you made a mistake, and I don't dispute that, but I can't go on like it never happened. I need you to talk to me, please."

I hand her the mug, and she takes a sip, looking at me expectantly while I rub the back of my neck before sitting down next to her at the end of the bed. "Okay. Well, you know how I told you that your dad, Gio, and I went to school together? Well, I had a fiancée in my last year. We'd been together for over a year, and I thought I was head over heels in love with the woman, as she was with me. I wasn't rich like Gio or Antony but was doing well enough for myself. I'd just started my first business, which I was running out of Gio's garage. It was around Christmas, and I bought a ring. I was going to propose, so I went to her house to surprise her and used my key to get in. Except I was the one who ended up being surprised... when I found her in bed with Antony. She's now your stepmom."

Maisie gasps and I offer her a forced smile.

"That sort of betrayal coming from two of the people I loved most in the world, combined with the fact that I grew up in foster care, meant that Christmas was never the celebration it should have been. I froze my heart after Monica. I guess that's the best way to describe it. I thought if my heart was cold, it couldn't get broken again—that *I* couldn't be broken. I could go on and live my life and run my business without having to feel. To make matters worse, I learned that Monica had also been taking business information and passing it along to Antony."

I sigh, running my fingers through my hair.

"So, when I saw you with him, in that corner, it looked like you and your father were conspiring against me. And I lost it. I'm not proud of what I did, what I said, or how I handled it, but I need you to understand that never once did I actually believe the vile words that came out of my mouth. I was just mad and hurt and desperately didn't want to be taken for a fool again. I started to thaw around you, and that made me feel vulnerable. I was trying to claw my way back to my sense of safety."

I hear Maisie sniffle, and look up to see that she's crying again.

"Baby, no tears." I pull her into my arms, and she cuddles close.

"I'm so sorry that happened to you. I'm so sorry." Her small hands cup my face, and she brushes the softest kisses against my lips.

"Well, I've made a decision. From now on, I'm going to have nothing but positive Christmas memories, starting with this one. Happy Christmas, Maisie, my love." Reaching into my pocket, I pull out an antique ring box, and Maisie slides off my lap to sit next to me.

"Jack..."

I cut her off by kneeling by the bed and opening the box to reveal her nan's ring—the same one the older woman had given me with her blessing when I met her yesterday at the care home. Maisie gasps, her hands coming up to cover her face in shock.

"I know we played the part for Marcus, but I need it for real, Maisie. I can't do this life without you. Your light, your smile, and your joy make every day a new adventure, and I never want to live in the dark again. Will you take this thawed heart and make it yours for the rest of time?"

"Yes!" Maisie tackles me back onto the floor, kissing me desperately as I try to set the ring on her finger. I manage to get it on before she gets my buckle undone. By the time her hand wraps around me, I'm already losing focus.

"Maisie. Love. Princess..." The feel of her small hand wrapped around my cock has me so hard there's no blood left for speaking. And when her tongue laps over the tip, I let out a surprised shout. "Love, you don't have—"

I moan as she slides me into her warm mouth. Fuck, she feels like heaven. Warm, satin heaven. I tangle a hand in her hair as she starts to slide up and down my shaft. My eyes cross when she hums as she hits the base and swallows. The feel of her throat working around me has me ready to blow in an embarrassingly short amount of time. I grit my teeth, counting back from twenty as she continues her assault on my cock.

Gripping the base, Maisie licks up to the head, staring at me the whole time. Just the way I like it, her warm brown eyes blazing with passion. I grab her arm and use both hands to tug her up and onto my lap before smacking her ass sharply.

"Ride me, Princess."

Maisie positions me at her entrance, slamming down in one sharp movement, and we both cry out. Her hips roll in a rhythm that should be illegal, and I grip them tightly as she continues to move over me. Her tits bounce, calling to me, so I reach up and pinch her nipple, and her walls tighten around me. She moans loudly, her nails digging into my chest as she leans forward for more leverage.

Gripping her hips again, I move her up and slam back into her from below. The wet sounds of our bodies are the only noise in the quiet room besides the panting. "Fuck, Princess, you feel so good. I need you to come for me. Come for me, Princess. I want to feel you dripping down on me."

Maisie's eyes glaze over as she continues to chase that high. I pinch her nipple with one hand and her clit with the other, and she comes undone with a sharp scream, her body twitching and convulsing above mine in a beautiful display of unbridled passion. When her pussy clamps around my shaft, I lose the tenuous hold I had, and I follow her over, filling her up until we're both breathless, sweaty, and lying on the carpet.

"I love you." I wrap my arms around her, pulling her close.

"I love you," Maisie whispers back.

Epilogue

Maisie

*O**ne year later***

"No. Not just no but fuck no!" My body is vibrating, my anger reaching its tipping point.

After Jack followed me home and proposed, it was a whirlwind of making up, making out, and making memories. Jack says it was the best three weeks of his life. Little does he know that I have a surprise that will top it. However, first, I have to deal with the man standing in front of me.

Antony, my sperm donor. *Not father.* He was never a father.

"What are you doing here?" I hiss while glaring in his direction.

"What do you mean *what am I doing here*? I'm your father. I'm going to walk you down the aisle."

I snort. First, there is no aisle. And second, there is no way this waste of oxygen is going to walk me anywhere. "I don't know how you found out about our wedding, or why you're here, but you need to leave, or I will have you removed from the premises."

"Mandy, I'm your father. It's my right to walk you down the aisle. I have a photographer all set up."

"Maisie," I interrupt him.

"Er, what?" The look of genuine confusion on his face has me shaking my head.

"My name is Maisie. You are not now—nor have you ever been—my father. And the last thing you will do is walk me down the aisle. I would rather step on Legos than take a photograph with you. Unfortunately for me, I don't have a father. I have you, my sperm donor. A real father would know their child's name."

Antony frowns at me, and I can tell by the tightening around his mouth I've made him angry. The funny thing is, I don't care. Maybe a year ago I would have, back when I still felt like a little girl desperate for her daddy's approval and love. Things changed, and I'm no longer that little girl. I'm the COO of a multi-million dollar company and a chief architect of what the papers are heading as the most significant merger of the decade. I don't need this man's approval anymore. I finally approve of myself.

I can tell Antony is gearing up for an argument when a hand clamps down on his shoulder, and he flinches. I smirk when I see my soon-to-be husband standing behind him.

"I believe my bride asked you to leave." Jack's tone brokers no arguments, and Antony glares at both of us before storming out of the room. Sighing, I turn back into Jack's arms and he leads me into the bridal suite.

We're getting married on the beach like Nan and Pops did. I'm wearing a tea-length white dress with spaghetti straps, perfect for sand and sun.

Marcus and Alexandra walk up, and I smile at them. They are the best thing to come out of this merger.

It was a few weeks after Jack proposed that I remembered the deal. When Jack explained what happened at the resort, how Marcus helped him pack up and return to New York to try to find me, I cried again. Then he told me that Alexandra said if he'd permanently fucked things up with me, he could kiss any deal he put forward without me as dead before the ink dried. Apparently, she thought I was the business genius between us. She also made sure to mention *happy spouse, happy house* and all that jazz.

Jack takes my hand, and I smile at him. Uncle Gio was supposed to be here, but he's somewhere in Texas and couldn't make it. While it hurts,

I'm sure something important is going on and whatever it is, I hope it sorts itself out quickly for his sake. The last time I talked to him, he wasn't his usual boisterous self. It was concerning, but he's adamant that he's fine and will send us a present for the honeymoon. Besides Uncle Gio, everyone important to us is in attendance. Jack opted to walk with me down the aisle, as a symbol of our unity.

"We will do this together, Princess. We're partners, which means we do everything together, starting with taking the first step toward our happily ever after."

I admit his words made me cry at the time, much to Jack's consternation.

***

"Hello, Mrs. Foster." Jack's arms slide around my waist, and I smile.

"Hello, Mr. Foster."

My new husband kisses my temple, and we stand to look out over the small group of friends and family as they laugh and eat amongst themselves.

"I have a present for you."

Jack turns me around in his arms. "We said no gifts, Princess."

I roll my eyes and raise a hand, showing off the diamond bracelet I woke up wearing this morning.

"What? Technically, it wasn't a wedding present! It was…" Jack fumbles over his words, likely trying to come up with an excuse, and I just raise an eyebrow until he gives up and grins. "Okay, so it was a wedding present. Sue me."

"Don't tempt me."

We both laugh. I open my satin clutch and pull out a small box tied with a blue ribbon.

"It was my something blue. Go ahead. Open it."

Jack looks at me before releasing the ribbon and lifting the lid from the box. His eyebrows dip until he realizes what he's looking at. He picks up the small white stick, and the box falls to the floor. He glances at the stick, at me, and then back at the stick again.

"Congratulations, Daddy."

That has his whole body jerking. He looks at me again, and I can see the tears swimming in his eyes. Jack pulls me against his chest, cradling me protectively.

"I love you. So much," he whispers, and I smile, accepting the kiss he presses to my lips. Then he steps back and lifts the stick high in the air. "I'm gonna be a father!" Jack declares to the entire room.

All I can hear are the laughs, happy squeals, and congratulations as we are mobbed by our friends and family. And I can't help but think this might be the best Christmas ever.

From the Author

Thank you for reading Jack Frost, CEO. I hope you love Jack and Maisie as much as I do. This book started as a demand from my PA, Gwen, and went from there. Writing Jack Frost was so much fun, and I hope you enjoyed this glimpse into their world. I always loved reading, and now I have a separate love of writing. I hope you stick around and watch this world grow with me. You can read more about Gio and Delilah in This is Growing Up- Wild Child Reckless Book One.

I am always looking to connect! You can find me in the following places.

SmutTok Made Me Do It Facebook Group

Juliet McKinleys Book Nook

Sign Up for my newsletter here so that you never miss a beat, giveaway or sneak peek-

Newsletter   julietmckinley.myflodesk.com

TikTok   @JulieyMcKinleyAuthor

Instagram@JulietMckinleyAuthor

Facebook Juliet McKinley

Also by-

<u>Wild Child Reckless Series</u>
This is Growing Up
This is Meant to Be*

<u>Novellas</u>
Jack Frost, CEO